ALSO BY BERNIE KEATING:

When America Does It Right.
AIIE Press, Atlanta, GA, 1978

Riding the Fence Lines: Riding the Fences That Define the Margins of Religious Tolerance.
BWD Publishing LLC, Toledo, OH, 2003

Buffalo Gap Frontier: Crazy Horse to NoWater to the Roundup.
Pine Hills Press, Sioux Falls, SD, 2008

1960's Decade of Dissent: The Way We Were.
Author House, Bloomington, IN, 2009

Songs and Recipes: For Macho Men Only.
Author House, Bloomington, IN, 2010

Rational Market Economics: A Compass for the Beginning Investor.
Author House Publishing, Bloomington, IN, 2010

Music: Then and Now
Author House Publishing, Bloomington, IN 2011

A Romp Thru Science: Plato and Einstein to Steve Jobs
Author House Publishing, Bloomington, IN 2013

Riding My Horse

Growing up in Buffalo Gap

By Bernie Keating

authorHOUSE®

AuthorHouse™
1663 Liberty Drive
Bloomington, IN 47403
www.authorhouse.com
Phone: 1-800-839-8640

Published by AuthorHouse 3/4/2013

ISBN: 978-1-4817-2365-7 (sc)
ISBN: 978-1-4817-2366-4 (hc)
ISBN: 978-1-4817-2367-1 (e)

Library of Congress Control Number: 2013903948

TABLE OF CONTENTS

LOOKING BACK

Looking back at those early years in Buffalo Gap, Scott realized learning to ride a horse and becoming a "real cowboy" was his rite-of-passage into manhood. By riding a horse, he learned how to stand on his own two feet. The experience was more than staying in the saddle and setting the direction for the horse to go, it was doing it with guts --with character.

His teachers were his parents, siblings, pioneer neighbors who had helped settle the "Last Frontier", and even Sioux Indian friends from the nearby Pine Ridge Indian Reservation.

With the outbreak of World War Two, Scott moved away with his family to live elsewhere. So did most everyone else in town. Buffalo Gap became deserted as a virtual ghost town, but his roots are still there; that heritage should serve him well. His childhood may be all in the past, but he has the memories of when he became a cowboy --a real man. Looking back at those years, he remembers when and how it all came into sync.

A REAL COWBOY?—AWESOME!

Scott was in a world of his own. For one thing, he wanted to be a cowboy like his friend, Rex. For another thing, he wanted to be a Sioux Indian like his friend, Swallow, but knew that was not going to happen because a guy cannot change from being a white kid into an Indian like that. But he could wish, anyway.

It was late on a summer night as he lay on his stomach in bed with the sheet drawn over his head like a tent, a flashlight in one hand and holding the book he was reading about a big day at a cattle roundup. Turning a page in the semi-darkness, he read:

> .. and then the horse Dakota Joe rode reared up on its hind legs, but the cowboy grabbed the saddle horn and kept in the saddle.

He dreamed about being a cowboy and riding a horse at a cattle roundup like the one Rex Norman's dad ran -- he owned a ranch with lots of cattle. Rex was learning to ride a horse and got to ride on one every day during the summer. That would be incredible!

"Scott, turn off that flashlight and get to sleep," his mother declared through the open door, raising her voice for emphasis. She knew he was hiding under the sheet reading his favorite book, but it was well past bedtime even for summer vacation. "Tomorrow is a busy day and I don't want you so tired in the morning you can't get out of bed. I need you to help me peel tomatoes for canning," she announced, as if Scott didn't know there was always canning to do every morning in the summer.

"Okay, Mother," he sighed, "but please, pretty please, can't I read for just five more minutes?" he pleaded. "I promise. I am almost to the end of a chapter."

"Five minutes, and no more," she responded with a voice of finality, knowing that otherwise this dialogue would continue. "Then it's lights out." Scott was a fine boy and well behaved, unlike her oldest son who was a problem child before he joined the navy and was now overseas; he was never a help during the summer canning season like Scott.

They lived in Buffalo Gap, a small town in the Black Hills nestled up against a ridge of steep cliffs where the prairie ended and the mountains started. The Black Hills actually began a mile west of town at the ridge where Calico Canyon and Knapp's canyon rose up from the prairie. Further to the north was the wide gap in the ridgeline that gives the town its name: Buffalo Gap. In olden days the gap was a passageway for buffalo to move during their seasonal migration from the barren prairie up into the green pastures of the mountains where they summered. A little stream, Beaver Creek, flowed down through the gap and meandered along cottonwood groves through the town of Buffalo Gap and on toward the Cheyenne River. The creek had good fishing in the springtime when it ran full with melting winter snow, but during the hot summer it became sluggish and fishing wasn't so good.

Scott liked to go fishing with his Dad, who was a fisherman and a very good one, too. His dad caught fish nearly every time when he could go out in the evening after his work was done at the bank. He often took Scott with him to carry his fish creel so his son could learn to fish. Frank McCormick was the Buffalo Gap banker. Sometimes he would hook a trout and hand the pole to Scott so he could fight the fish and land it on the bank. Scott was thrilled. Then the next day his Dad would tell everyone in town about the big fish Scott had caught and brag that his son was a good fisherman. It made Scott real proud.

Tomorrow was going to be a special day, at least in the afternoon after his little sister and brother and he finished peeling the tomatoes. His playmate, Rex Norman, was coming into Buffalo Gap from the ranch to spend a few days with his Aunt Florence and Bill Sewright. Rex's mother and Aunt Florence were sisters. Rex was nine, one year older than Scott, but they were good friends because he spent time in the summer with the

Sewright's who owned the ranch across the dirt road from Scott's home. He looked from his front porch across the road at horses in the corral and beyond them at the barns and corrals where Bill Sewright kept his milk cows during the night. The cows spent their days on a pasture a mile east of town where the rancher herded them every morning and back to the ranch every night to be milked.

Bill Sewright was a special friend and Scott often followed the rancher throughout the day. The Sewright's only son, Floyd, had been killed five years before in a flash flood, and the rancher seemed to welcome the company of a boy. Floyd called his dad 'Pop Bill', and the name began to be used by all the other kids in the neighborhood. Bill Sewright was known around town as "Pop Bill".

Tomorrow would be a special day because Pop Bill had promised that this summer Rex and Scott could ride horses and herd the milk cows to the pasture in the morning and back to the ranch every evening for milking. It would be the first time Scott had ever been allowed to ride his own horse. Even though Pop Bill would accompany them in his pickup, the boys would be riding their own horses and actually herding the cows. That would be cool. Scott turned off his flashlight and thought of the big day ahead.

After peeling tomatoes in the morning, Scott rushed across the road to the Sewright ranch where he awaited the Norman's arrival. They parked their pickup in the driveway and Rex bounded out from the pickup's back deck where he had been riding.

"Hello, Scott!" shouted Rex as he jumped over the tailgate and raced to where his friend stood beside Pop Bill and Aunt Florence.

"Hello, Rex!" responded a happy Scott. Even though they knew each other from their time together last summer, it was kind of like they were strangers meeting again for the first time since it had been so long since they had seen each other. Then again, Rex was a couple inches tall than he was last summer and looked different. They did not see each other during the winter months because Rex lived on the ranch twenty miles east of Buffalo Gap in the Cheyenne River country and went to a county school. Their fathers saw a lot of each other in business because as the banker, Scott's dad had a lot of business with all the ranchers, but it was done down town in the bank, and Rex who went to the country school on Harrison Flat seldom came to Buffalo Gap with his father. So being somewhat shy and timid around strangers, Scott seemed to be greeting Rex again for the first time. "Are you going to stay here in Buffalo Gap with your uncle?"

"Yeah," Rex answered with some hesitation. "I think so. Uncle Bill and Aunt Florence said it would be okay, but Dad and Mother always seem to think I'd be some sort of bother to them. Gosh, you'd think by now they would be happy to let me spend some time with my Aunt and Uncle Bill."

"I hope you can stay. We can play in the corrals and the loft of the hay barns, and maybe Pop Bill will even help us saddle horses and do some riding. That would be cool."

"Yeah, I ride horses on the ranch all the time with my dad, but I never have anyone to ride with. It will be fun if you and I can go riding together."

"I hope I can ride Buck. He's my favorite horse."

"Which one is Buck?"

"He is the light colored buckskin with the brown spot on his nose."

"Is he broke good."

"Yeah, real good! When Floyd was alive before he drowned, he used to ride Buck. It was his favorite horse, too, just like he's my favorite."

"Well that's good. A horse needs to be broke good; otherwise he can start bucking and sometimes even start on a runaway."

"Buck would never do that. Pop Bill would not let a kid ride a horse that was not broke good. Do you know how to put a saddle on a horse?"

"Yeah, I know how to do it, but saddles are so heavy that I need help from my dad to lift it up to the back of the horse. My dad usually puts on the blanket and lifts the saddle up, and then he lets me cinch it up. He says every cowboy needs to know how to cinch-up a saddle so it won't roll sideways and is safe for the cowboy to ride, and not too tight and uncomfortable for the horse."

"I've never cinched-up a saddle. Maybe you can show me how this summer. Are you going to stay in the same upstairs bedroom at the Sewright's where you stayed last summer?"

"Yeah, I suppose so. Sometimes it seems a bit scary upstairs in that bedroom all alone with only Uncle Bill and Aunt Florence in the house and no one else, and then I think about Floyd. That was Floyd's bedroom before he was drowned in the flood, so sometimes I think about that, wondering if he's still around somewhere looking down at me."

"Yeah, I loved Floyd! I miss him so much. He used to drive the pickup and let me sit in the front seat right beside him."

Floyd, the only son of Bill and Florence Sewright, was swept away in a flash flood five years before. He was twenty and the pride of his parents, who never fully recovered from their loss – perhaps never would. Summer had become a sentimental time when they were able to have their nephew, Rex, come to stay with them for a few weeks, sleeping in Floyd's bedroom, and spending his days shadowing his uncle, Pop Bill, as he went about the day's work on the ranch. Florence never mentioned it, but she knew having boys with her husband during the summer while he was working was one of the few pleasures in life he still had.

Buffalo Gap was a small town but spread-out and included a couple ranches on the out skirts of town like that of Bill Sewright's. It had been one of the first pioneer settlements in the Black Hills when Buffalo Gap started as a stage coach station soon after gold was discovered further north in Custer and Deadwood. Some of the men in town were early pioneers who drove cattle herds north from Texas toward Montana and decided to stay in the local area and become ranchers. Scott's neighbor, Gene Griffis, came as a cowboy, then got his own ranch, and later became Deputy Sheriff. That was fifty years earlier, and now the pioneers were hunched-over old men, walking with canes, whose best days were in the past. A half dozen of them spent most hours during summer sitting on the bench in the shade under the awning in front of Frenchie's saloon talking about times of the past. There was usually a game of horseshoes in progress alongside the saloon for them to watch.

The main street in town came from the north, turned left at the main intersection and headed east across the railroad tracks, over the Beaver Creek Bridge, and then climbed up the hill and east out of town. At the main intersection was a red sandstone building that was Frank McCormick's bank. It was the principle business in town. All the businesses were located on Main Street. Across from the bank was Phillip's grocery store and Mel's Service Station. Next door was Bert Dowdy's barber shop and a half block further east was Degnan's grocery story run by John and Nettie Degnan. With so many ranchers coming to town to shop, the town even had a third grocery store run by Frank Towers. In the other direction north from the bank was the Buffalo Gap Gazette, the Bell telephone exchange where Anna Swick was the telephone operator who connected all the local phone calls and plugged in for long distance.

Frenchie's pool hall run by Julius Gerber came next. Across the street north of Frenchie's was the post office and Charlie Streeter's shop where he made saddles. They were the only saddles ranchers and the cowboys of the region would ride because they were fitted and hand-crafted by Charlie with his emblem stamped into every saddle: C.G. Streeter. He hand-made them perfect to fit each cowboy individually. If you kept going north past the saddle shop and a couple vacant lots, you'd come to the Bill Sewright ranch home and beyond it to his corrals and barns. Scott's home was across the dirt road west of the Sewright ranch, and further north was another ranch that belonged to Art Kroth. West of town there was nothing but sage brush and prairie for a mile until you came to the opening of Calico Canyon and the steep front ridge of the Black Hills. Yes, Buffalo Gap may be a small town, but it was the only place where Scott had lived, and he loved it.

Next afternoon, Pop Bill called Scott and Rex who were playing in the hay lofts over the horse stables to come to the corral.

"Boys, I've got some work for you to help me with," he announced in a matter-of-fact voice as if it was something routine.

"Do you want to help me shovel the horse manure out of the horse stables," he asked in a serious tone of voice at the same time he had a trace of a smile on his face.

Rex and Scott were stunned and stood in silence. They had a feeling that this might be a joke, but played along with Pop Bill.

"Okay, since you don't want to do any shoveling, perhaps you will help me saddle some horses and ride up to the pasture to get some cattle," and then he laughed.

"Yeah!" yelled Scott at the top of his voice. He was elated. This was what he had been waiting for all summer.

"Pop Bill, I knew you were kidding," declared Rex smugly.

Bill told them it was time to saddle-up and they could go with him to the pasture to bring the cows back to the ranch for milking. There were five horses running free in the corral. They were not easy to catch since they were seldom ridden. The tallest horse was solid white with a black streak along its back. His name was *Whitey*. Scott's horse was buckskin named *Buck*. He was colored a light tan that fit his name. Rex's horse was a red-tinted sorrel mare named *Red* that was such a dark red that in the evening when the sun was going down she seemed almost black.

With the two boys trailing alongside him, Pop Bill could not approach the horses because they were so skittish, so he went to the harness shed next to the horse barn and got a lariat to rope his horse. He asked the boys to hang back since the horses were spooked by having strangers with him. Then he was able to approach within a few feet of Whitey and simply drop the noose over Whitey's head around his neck. When he tried to place a halter on its head, the horse raised his neck up too high for him to reach.

"Come on boy, don't do that to me," Pop Bill whispered softly to the horse. "Rex and Scott are coming with me, and we cowboys are going out to round-up some cattle. I know you're scarred with all the excitement here, but settle down," he murmured to the horse in a soft voice, but also speaking to the two boys at his side who would like to be identified as cowboys. He held his hand to whitey's nose and gently rubbed it and placed a hand on his neck and gently pulled it down while he placed the halter behind the ear.

"That's a good horse. Now, cowboys, we're making some headway," he announced to the two boys who stood behind him. Taking hold of the halter rope, he led Whitey back to the saddle shed that contained the saddles, bridles, lariats, harness for work horses, and other ranch equipment. Tying the halter rope to the hitching post beside the door, he placed a bridle bit into the horse's mouth and pulled the bridle over the halter. He laid the saddle blanket over the horse's back and spread it out smooth. Then he lifted the saddle over the blanket and undid the stirrup and cinch free of the saddle horn so they could fall to the other side of the horse. Reaching under the belly of the horse, he pulled the cinch toward him and buckled it up.

"Boys, it is important to cinch-up a saddle correctly," he instructed as he demonstrated the procedure. "The cinch holds the saddle firmly in place on the horse's back so it does not roll to the side with the cowboy if the horse starts to buck or suddenly turns when running fast, but it is also necessary to hold the saddle in place when a cowboy is roping and has to hitch his rope around the saddle horn to keep a taunt line on a calf. If a cowboy ropes something and loops it around the saddle horn, the saddle and cowboy could go flying off into space because it is the cinch that holds the saddle to the horse. So remember that boys. Always pay attention to the right way to cinch-up a saddle on a horse." Then he paused and remembered to add more instructions. "But don't pull the cinch too tight across the belly of a horse because it might cause the horse some

9

discomfort or even make it hard for the horse to breathe if it is running fast and needs all the air it can get. So, Boys, that is your first lesson about how to cinch-up a horse."

Scott and Rex were listening intently.

"Thanks, Pop Bill. My dad told me all about that. I've learned how to cinch-up my horse out on the ranch," boasted Rex with a knowing reply that implied he already knew all that stuff. "I do it that way all the time. There is a right way to be a good cowboy, and my dad has taught me all about it."

Pop Bill responded, "Rex, your dad is a good cowboy, so I'll bet he told you lots of important things about horses. Isn't that so?" Bill knew that some boys at that age tended to be a bit arrogant. Rex seemed to be like his father, Bill Sewright's brother-in-law. Joe Norman was a good man and excellent rancher, but he was also arrogant, conceited, and acted superior when around other ranchers, even during the business dealings that Joe and Bill had together. His son, Rex, apparently came by it naturally, or perhaps it was a reflection of the ranch environment in which he was raised. When he was young, his own son, Floyd, was a little like that, but as he became a teenager, he out-grew it, no doubt, the result of the influence of his mother.

"Yes, Pop Bill, he's told me lots of stuff."

With the boys at his side, Pop Bill was able to approach Buck, get a halter on him, and lead him back to the harness shed to be saddled.

"Now, Scott, you might not have saddled a horse before so let me show you how." He went into the harness shed and carried out a saddle blanket and saddle. He carried the blanket very carefully folded over his arm as if it were some sort of a special artifact. "First, the blanket goes on the back of the horse and gets spread out with no wrinkles that could create a sore on the horse's back under the saddle."

"Wow!" said Scott. "That's certainly a beautiful saddle blanket. It looks brand new like it's never been used before."

"Well, Scott, this used to be Floyd's. It was a birthday present. I gave it to him on his twentieth birthday just before he was drowned. I guess no one has used it since, but I don't see any sense in saving it any longer." As he said this, he spread the blanket carefully on the horse's back, patted it so it lay smooth; and leaned momentarily against Buck with his arms stretched over the horse's back, turning his face away from the boys. The sight of Floyd's blanket that had remained unused since his death created a sudden heartache he had not anticipated. He momentarily teared-up, paused for a minute, took a deep breath, and then recovered himself and reached down for the saddle that lay at his feet.

"Scott, a saddle is heavy. It may be too heavy for you to lift up to the back of a horse, so let me show you how to do it. In fact, I do it this way myself sometimes." He then demonstrated by leaning the saddle against the side of the horse and pushing it upward until it fell in place on the back of the horse. "Scott, I'll take the saddle off again and let you try it once yourself."

It did not look easy to Scott, but he did his best and on the second try gradually got the saddle up atop of Buck. Then reaching under the belly, he reached for the cinch which hung on the other side and pulled it through and with some difficulty managed to bucket it together.

"Pop Bill, is that about the right amount of pressure to tighten the cinch?" he asked, but knew he had done it exactly as he had been instructed.

"Yeah, Scott. That seems about right. You are a quick learner," he said praising the young boy. Scott felt real good. He was learning how to be a cowboy.

Then they caught the sorrel horse for Rex and led her back to the harness shed to be saddled. Rex took over and immediately grabbed the horse blanket and with some difficulty reached it up to the back of Red and spread it out. Pop Bill helped smooth out the wrinkles. Rex was a strong boy and had saddled a horse before, so he was able to push the saddle up the side of Red exactly as Pop Bill had demonstrated and it fell atop the horses back. He pulled the cinch and stirrup free of the saddle horn so they could fall on the backside of the horse. Reaching under the belly of the horse, he grabbed the cinch and buckled it up.

"Good job, Rex," commended Pop Bill. "Exactly the way it should be done." Rex and Scott would be good company for the summer. "Okay, Boys, take ahold the reins of your horse and lead them over to the gate."

The boys followed Pop Bill to the gate that led out of the corral.

"Now let me show you something about getting on a horse," Pop Bill continued. "You always mount a horse from the left side."

"Why from the left side," questioned Scott.

"Everyone knows that," chided Rex. "It's because every cowboy always does it that way and the horse expects it."

"Well, that is partially true," responded Pop Bill in a reassuring tone.

"It is because most cowboys are right handed, and they have better control of the horse when getting on if they do it from the left side. You take the reins in the left hand and grab ahold of the saddle horn. Then place your left boot in the stirrup, your right hand on the back of the saddle and pull yourself up, swinging your right leg over the saddle and into the stirrup on the other side. Here let me show you how it's done." So he mounted Whitey, and then got back off again.

"It can be difficult for a young boy with a tall horse to reach the stirrup with his left leg, and it even gets difficult sometimes for me to do when I have hurt my leg or when I'm tired. Let me show you a way you can always count on to get on a horse." Then he led Whitey over to the rail fence and demonstrated how to climb part way up on the fence and stand on a rail, then lift the right leg up and slide over onto the saddle.

"So, getting on a tall horse gets easy to do. Never worry if you have trouble reaching your foot up to the stirrup. There will always be a rail fence or a boulder or something that you can climb on and slide over into the saddle." Scott felt good to know that, because he'd be embarrassed if he was ever unable to get on his horse.

"Okay, Boys, time to head to the pasture to get the cows. I'll help you mount up this first time," said Pop Bill. He reached for Scott's left leg and lifted it up so he could reach the stirrup with his foot, then grabbing the saddle horn, swung his right foot over and he was suddenly sitting in the saddle – like a real cowboy.

"I can do it by myself. I've done it lots of times before," boasted Rex. He slowly lifted his left leg and with considerable effort on the third try was finally able to reach the stirrup with his foot. He grabbed the saddle horn, pulling himself up and swung his right foot over the saddle.

Suddenly, his sorrel horse, Red, jumped to the right and reared up on its hind legs, then began bucking as it jumped from the front to hind feet in a quick jerking motion. It happened so suddenly and was such a jarring thing that it wrenched a surprised Rex from his saddle and he flew off the horse and onto the ground in a heap. His horse ran off to the side.

Pop Bill went to the aid of Rex, and helped him to his feet. "Are you hurt any?" he asked. Rex stood still in a daze.

"No, I guess I'm okay, but what happened?" asked Rex as he steadied himself. "That is the first time I've ever been bucked off a horse, and it sure wasn't fun."

"Well, Rex, it may have been the first time, but it won't be the last time," said Pop Bill with a smile. "It happens now and then to every cowboy. Floyd used to get bucked off. Old Red just got nervous with a new cowboy on her back and did what she knows best to do. Here, I'll help you get back on."

Pop Bill retrieved the reins of Red, and patted her nose and shoulders to calm her down and whispered to her softly to get her settled. Then he lifted the left leg of Rex so his foot could reach the stirrup and helped him into the saddle. Rex was glad for the help this time. Pop Bill opened the gate of the corral, mounted his own horse, Whitey, and led the way out.

Now they were real cowboys on their way to roundup some cattle. Scott was excited -- It was awesome!

"SCOTT, ARE WE LOST?"

Scott had been in Calico Canyon before; it was the Christmas before his older brother joined the navy. Dennis was his role model – he could do anything. That year he led Scott, Betty, Billy and Edwin up into Calico Canyon to get the family Christmas tree and drag it home over the frozen snow.

Hiking the mile through snow drifts across the prairie to Calico Canyon was easy; they were used to hiking in the snow. The canyon gorge opened up into a wide chasm between cliffs that rose on both sides. The ruts of a road led inside to an abandoned quarry; the sandstone from that quarry with its swirl of reddish-purple color was what gave Calico Canyon its name. The stones were used to build the bank, schoolhouse, and other buildings in Buffalo Gap. The road dead- ended at the quarry and the canyon narrowed leaving a nearly impenetrable thicket of rocks and trees on the gorge bottom.

They found a perfect Christmas tree, and Dennis tied the tree with a rope so they could drag it back to Buffalo Gap. It was an eight-foot spruce but easy to drag on top the snow with Dennis in the lead. That was the first time Scott had been in Calico Canyon. It was shadowy and foreboding, but a place he wanted to visit again.

On Christmas morning, Scott's parents gave him and Billy their first BB gun. Wow! Scott was excited – his first real gun. He had to share ownership with his brother, but that was no problem because Billy, age six, could hardly hold it high enough to aim, and for sure he wasn't strong enough to pump it and re-load.

Christmas morning there were patches of snow on the ground, but a wind had blown it clear in most places; so, Scott convinced his dad that he and Billy should try out their new gun and take it west of town on the prairie for a hike. They would not be long and back in time for Christmas dinner in the late afternoon. Mother was busy in the kitchen so Scott did not bother her, and anyway, a gun and a hike was a Dad's business.

"Okay, boys, but your mother will have a big Christmas dinner ready to serve at three, so you get back long before then. Okay?"

"Thanks, Dad, we'll be back in plenty of time," Scott responded with the best of intentions.

"And remember," cautioned his Dad, "Always keep the gun on safety when you are walking, and never point it at anyone even if it is not loaded. Always keep the barrel pointed either up into the sky or down at the ground."

"Yes, Dad, I remember that is how you taught us. We will be careful."

They hiked west of town onto the prairie toward the mountains, and then it occurred to Scott to visit the quarry in Calico Canyon where they could take target practice with the BB gun. When they got there, they found the bottom of the canyon was heavy with snow, so they climbed up above the quarry near the mountain top where the snow had melted. Scott loved to explore. He found a deer trail through the trees with fresh deer tracks and decided to follow the tracks in the hope they might see a deer. That would be cool. The trail was easy to follow and after a quarter of a mile gradually led downward until they found themselves near the bottom of the canyon and in heavy snow. Trudging through snow two feet deep, Scott decided they should climb up on the south side of the canyon wall where the snow might be lighter. After hiking for a while, that did not seem a good idea because the south side with a northern exposure got no sun and also had heavy snow; so, they dropped down to the canyon bottom again, trudged through the heavy snow and climbed up the north side of the canyon with a sunny southern exposure and lighter snow coverage. They scrambled along the canyon wall midway between the top of the mountain and the bottom of the canyon, but there was no trail and it was slow slogging.

At that point, Scott realized it was getting late if they were going to be on time for the Christmas dinner. If they hurried maybe they could still make it. Unfortunately, they ran into a vertical ledge that prevented going further in that direction. Deciding to follow their tracks in the snow backwards, they climbed toward the top of the canyon wall to get over the top of the ledge. Looking up, they saw a cliff above that prevented that. The only alternative route was to go back down to the canyon bottom.

On the Calico Canyon bottom, Scott could barely push his way through snow that came up to his waist, and Billy was in worse trouble and unable to move; the snow came up to his armpits. Reaching back, Scott grabbed his arms pulling him forward. After a half hour of fighting the deep snow, they left the canyon bottom and found that a hundred feet up the side there was lighter snow and the semblance of a deer trail. They climbed upward, eventually reaching the top of the rock quarry. Now Scott knew exactly where they were; near the entrance to Calico Canyon, but he also knew it was already long past the time for the Christmas dinner. It was getting dark. Billy was exhausted. Scott was tired, but worse than that, he knew they were in serious trouble at home. What was supposed to be a short hike with their new BB gun had turned into a personal disaster. He led the way as rapidly as two dog-tired boys could hustle across the mile of prairie to Buffalo Gap.

On the back porch they took off cold wet boots and cautiously entered the back door, fearing the worse. Then a surprise: the house seemed empty.

"Hello, anybody home!" Scott called.

"In here, boys," responded his dad who sat alone in the front room.

"Dad, where is everybody?" Scott asked, fearing the response.

"They are all out on the prairie west of town in the car searching everywhere for you boys. Mother took everyone with her, even the Streeter boys, and they are driving up and down the prairie in the car blowing whistles, yelling, honking horns, and trying to find you. What happened, are you hurt?"

"No Dad, but we ran into heavy snow in Calico Canyon and got delayed." Scott said it meekly and hoped that response would work.

"Calico Canyon! What were you doing in Calico Canyon? That dangerous gorge is not a safe place for two boys in the dead of winter."

"We went to the rock quarry to do some shooting practice with our new BB gun, but followed a deer trail and it led us into heavy snow."

"Well, boys, maybe I can understand that, but if I were you, I would not try to use that explanation with your mother. She will be furious. Maybe you should just tell her you got lost and did not know where you were until it was too late and getting dark. Then beg her forgiveness and promise to never do it again."

Mother dashed into the house in tears. Even before she could say a word or speak, Dad told her the boys had safely returned, cold, wet, and exhausted, and were resting in the bedroom. He told her they had gotten disoriented and a little lost. He said he had bawled them out and given a tongue-lashing, and was sure they had learned their lesson and would never do it again. Mother was sobbing, in tears, and didn't know whether to cry in joy or be angry. Dad had saved the day for Scott and Billy.

In all the following years of growing up, that evening was his Dad's finest hour – the best memory Scott ever had. His dad had become his partner in a misdeed cover-up to help survive the aftermath of a horrible afternoon experience; and his Dad assumed a new lofty plateau in Scott's affection -- becoming his lifetime buddy. Scott endured one of his worse times ever, but that Christmas Day was humbling and one he would never forget.

4

"YOU'RE RIDING MY PONY!"

Scott and Swallow rode their ponies down the ravine into Beaver Creek, waded across with water to the horses knees, and entered the No-Water encampment on the Sewright ranch. The old grandfather, called No-Water, reclined alongside his tipi and watched as the boys dismounted. He wore a solitary eagle feather in his hair that hung long and straight, smiled, and said something in the Lakota language to his grandson.

"What did he say, Swallow?" Scott quizzed his friend since he understood only a few words in the Indian language.

"He said in the old days when they lived here with Chief Sitting Bull, he had a pinto pony exactly like yours. He's always talking about the old days and the crazy things they worshipped. It's boring. Come on. Let's go over to the hay barns and play," responded Swallow who was bi-lingual from his time in the Reservation school.

Swallow was Scott's playmate for the summer. He lived on the Pine Ridge Indian Reservation. During the winter the family had little income, living in poverty like nearly all the other families on the Reservation; one of their salvations came from Bill Sewright who brought meat, potatoes, and other food to the reservation and traded them in exchange for the men to work during the summer on his ranch in Buffalo Gap. Swallow's father, George No-Water, ran a few cattle on an isolated mesa on the reservation, called Cuny Table. While not as destitute as most Indian families, they lived in borderline poverty and George was happy to exchange summer work in exchange for winter provisions.

George was a mixed-blood Sioux with high status on the reservation, but even he was in need of help during the winter to ward-off the dire effects of poverty that all Indians found themselves with; a proud man, he knew he had to compromise his status to provide for his family and drove a team of workhorses to pull mowing machines for Sewright during the haying season

Sewright hustled any way he could, a struggling rancher barely keeping his head above water during the rough Depression Years of the 1930's. One of his enterprises was to butcher pigs, sheep and cows during the wintertime and take them with other provisions to the Indian reservation to sell. But he didn't actually sell anything because the destitute Indians had nothing. It was a bartering process. He'd give them meat, and provisions, and in return they'd agree to work on his ranch the following summer when he'd supply them with food and a place to stay.

The Francis Stands-alone family of four spent the summer living in an abandoned railroad box car that had been moved to the vacant lot across from Scott's house in Buffalo Gap. Several males: Percy-Kills-a-Warrior, Comes-Again, and John Sitting-Bull, would come without their families and live in a shack that was once a hay barn. They had been warriors in the Battle of the Little Bighorn against General Custer sixty years before when they were teenagers.

The No-Water family pitched a tipi a mile north of the town alongside Beaver Creek. The tipi was supported with poles but covered with canvas since buffalo hides were no longer available. A rock enclosed fire pit was located in front of the tipi. The wagon they used for transportation from the reservation sat nearby. A Squaw-Cooler made with four poles that held a roof of pine boughs provided shade, and Swallow's mother and sister could be seen working under it.

Swallow's sister approached Scott after he had dismounted.

"You're riding my pony," she declared in a threatening voice and stood with a hostile hands-on-hips posture face-to-face directly in front of him. He was startled! How to respond to this angry girl?

"Gosh! I wouldn't have ridden the pony if I knew you'd be upset. Swallow said it would be okay."

"Well it's not," she retorted angrily. "No one rides my pony without asking, and me saying so."

She was a pretty girl about the same age as Scott with long uncombed black hair that fell loosely to her shoulders, high cheekbones, the light colored skin of a mixed-blood Indian, attractive dark piercing eyes, and a wide mouth that would look great with a smile; but she was not smiling. She wore a brightly colored blouse that seemed to Scott to be over-dressed for a tipi Indian encampment.

"I don't blame you for being mad. Swallow said I could ride the pony. Thank you for letting me ride, even if I didn't have your permission; and I'm sorry if you wanted to ride him too. He's a fine pony," Scott replied in as gracious a voice as possible having just been censured by this girl who stood in front of him with her hands on her hips in an unsympathetic manner, or at least it seemed that way to him.

"She's not a *he*," she retorted sharply. "My pony is named Paint and she is a mare. Don't you know a mare when you see one?"

He wondered how to get out of this conflict. "Are you Swallow's sister? What's your name?"

"Meadowlark," she responded harshly.

"Meadowlark. That is a pretty name. I like it. Meadowlark and Swallow, I guess your family likes bird names?"

"I like my name," she said curtly. Then her tone softened, and he saw the trace of a smile. If he maintained his cool and kept talking, maybe she would soften. "What is your name?" she asked.

"My name is Scott. I was named after my grandfather. Scott is not as a good a name as Meadowlark, but that's what my parents named me. I really like your name, Meadowlark."

"My brother is a year older than me, but I will be ten next month. I'm in the fifth grade and Swallow is a year ahead of me in school."

"Where do you go to school?"

"At the country school on Cuny Table.

"How many are in your class?"

"Only me and one other, but all the grades are in the same room.

"Wow! Eight grades in the same room and only one teacher?"

"Yes. But some of the grades have no students, so there are only ten in the school. How old are you?"

"I'm ten."

"Then you and I are the same age. How many are in your class?"

"We have six, four girls and me and another guy. But we only have

21

three grades in the same room. My teacher is a man and he is also my scoutmaster."

"What's a scoutmaster?"

"Well, it's kind of difficult to explain. We have ten boys in a Boy Scout troop, and he is our leader."

"Why do you have a troop, what do you do?"

"We go on hikes, go camping, and learn to tie knots, things like that. In the wintertime we have meetings, but we don't have any during the summer.

"What is camping?"

"It's where we hike somewhere for a night and sleep in a tent and cook our meals over a campfire. It's fun"

"Well, that doesn't sound like fun to me. Sounds like the same thing we do here during the summer when my Dad has to work on the Sewright ranch. If you think that's fun, then you must be crazy"

"I guess the difference is that we do it for fun, kind of like the early pioneers did. Meadowlark, maybe you don't like living here in a tipi, but it seems to me like it would be fun?"

"No, it's kind of boring out here all day with only my mother to talk to. I'd rather be on the Reservation in our home where I have lots of friends to play with. My friend Sally has a doll with eyes and lips that move and lots of dresses we can keep changing."

"Well, I don't like playing with dolls, so I guess I'd find that boring. Where do you live?"

"We live on Cuny Table."

"I know where that is. I've been there with my dad."

"Why were you there? What does your dad do?"

"He runs the bank."

"Runs the bank -- Wow! You folks must be rich."

"No, we're poor just like everyone else. At least if we're rich I sure don't know it, because we scrimp and save like everyone else. Mom patches all my brother's clothes and I get all the hand-me-downs to wear. She makes all my sister's dresses and don't buy store-bought clothes; so if we're rich someone forgot to tell my dad."

"Do you have a girlfriend?" Her tone was now very friendly and forgiving.

"No. None of the girls in my class are pretty. Do you have a boyfriend?"

"No, john Kills-a-Warrior asked me to be his girlfriend, but I don't like him. He is a bully and treats little kids mean during recess."

Swallow came up to stand beside Scott.

"Meadowlark," he cut in, "I told Scott he could ride your pony, so don't be so cranky. Scott, don't pay any attention to her. Come on, let's head to the barns."

Swallow's grandfather was an old man in his eighties long past the age of working on a ranch, and he sat all day in the shade under the cottonwood trees near the tipi. While he understood English when he wanted to, he seldom spoke anything but Lakota, and gradually Scott learned some of it. When the boys struck his fancy, he would tell them stories about the old days. Often Scott would linger with the grandfather by the campfire and listen to an old man with many memories about a nomad life on the plains that no one else wanted to hear.

The grandfather had been raised as a member of Chief Sitting Bull's tribe which roamed this country as nomads, living in tipi villages, and following the buffalo herds. This gap in the mountains was their home when the buffalo herds were leaving the Black Hills with the first snows, and moving onto the plains where the snow drifts were lighter. The Indians pitched their tipis along the creek in these cottonwood groves and feasted on the plentiful buffalo. Then later in winter, the tribe would move with the meandering herd out onto the plains and hunker down in protected ravines, sheltered from the blizzards that blew around the north end of *pah-HA SAH-pah*, the Black Hills.

No-Water was a survivor. He had been with Sitting Bull at the Little Bighorn when Custer's men attacked their village. That was sixty years earlier when he was a young warrior. It was a confused battle with women, children, warriors and soldiers everywhere. After the battle, No-Water fled with Chief Sitting-Bull into Canada. A few years later he returned with his wife and children to the reservation. There, they began a life of survival in a meager existence in the barren Badlands of Dakota.

Stories of his nomad life were told to Scott over the campfire as the old grandfather turned hunks of meat on a crude spit. When he felt like talking, words came forth in a combination of Lakota and his blend of English. Scott understood most of it, and Swallow translated the rest.

"Did he ever go up into *pah-HA SAH-pah* when he was a boy?" Scott quizzed him. The answer was a resounding *'no'*. Those mountains were a hostile place where few Indians ventured except in an armed hunting party. It was full of bears and other prey that attacked them and spooked their horses -- and then there was the thunder and lightning. The old warrior's eyes closed as he mumbled something about great spirits. Once he had climbed to the top of *mah-TOH pah-HA*, the mountain now called Bear Butte. There, No-Water was close to those spirits, and he saw visions of the White Buffalo. A cloud came and thunder cracked as lightning struck the trees. He fled in fear down the mountain in the rainstorm, never to return.

No-Water was telling Scott of this vision and these spirits as he continued to turn the spit over the fire. Swallow's father returned from his day on the ranch and told Scott he must go home before his parents worried, because a thunderstorm was on the way.

The storm hit. Lightning bolts glanced off the high peaks, turning night into day. Thunderclaps shook the foundations of Scott's house as the rain fell, and the wind uprooted trees which crashed to the ground outside his bedroom window.

Were these No-Water's angry spirits? Was No-Water's vision of a White Buffalo an angry God? Scott felt he could believe in the grandfather's Indian vision just as he did in the white man's church God he heard about on Sundays.

The storm passed and Scott snuggled under his warm blankets. He wondered what it was like when No-Water lived in a tipi village here in this Buffalo Gap many years ago. It was a dream that seemed very real to Scott.

In his dream, Scott was in the same Buffalo Gap long ago with No-Water and his tribe of Indians.

When morning came, No-Water awakened in a silent world except for the breathing of his *WEEN-yon*, Black Buffalo Woman, and their baby who huddled together under the buffalo robe in a darkened tipi, while outside the world was encased in snow and bitter cold at the beginning of the Dakota winter season.

No-Water and his small band of warriors arrived yesterday carrying their rolled-up tipis and possessions on travois' behind their horses. They knew buffalo would be on the move with the first snow of winter, migrating from the mountains of *pah-HA SAH-pah* onto the plains where buffalo spent the winter. Driving buffalo up a bluff, they would stampede the herd and chase them over a steep buffalo jump. As the injured buffalo tumbled down, warriors would be waiting at the bottom, using arrow and tomahawks to kill the struggling animals. No-Water's tribe could feast on fresh meat; the women would scrape the buffalo hides for capes and tipi covers, and prepare for the long winter ahead.

No-Water's band returned to each year when the buffalo were on the move -- both in the spring when the buffalo migrated up into *pah-HA SAH-pah* -- and again in the fall when they migrated down with the first snowfall. Now the women pulled down the tipis, loading all their possessions on travois' behind their horses. A new encampment was set up in a ravine near the Cheyenne River where the buffalo herds also spent the winter.

When spring came, they would travel three days north *to mah-TOH pah-HA*, Bear Butte, the center of their tribal culture where they would parlay with other tribes. Sitting Bull would be there. They would discuss many things, but the urgent subject would be traveling of white men though their Indian lands; they must discuss what should be done. This was Indian land and white men had no right to disturb the buffalo herds. Should they fight and kill the white man?

After the peace pipe had been smoked and the parlay of chieftains completed, the feast began and was followed by war dances that continued around the huge fire until early morning. It was a time of celebration in the shadow of *pah-Ha SAH-pah*: their beloved Black Hills homeland.

It was a nice dream, and Scott snuggled under the blanket in his warm bed. Then his mind changed to the beautiful girl, Meadowlark, and he hoped he would see her again.

5

THE ADMIRAL ORDERED
SCOTT TO ATTACK!

Summer vacation became boring. Scott was lonely. Yesterday Rex went back to his ranch so he had no playmate and there was nothing to do. Summer became a dreary time. Without Rex to accompany him, he could not herd Pop Bill's milk cows to the pasture by himself. Some days Pop Bill would let Scott ride Buck and go with him, but other times there was nothing to do. Darrel Thompson who was in his class and lived on the other side of town wasn't much fun. They played together during the school year at recess time, but Darrel was a bully and cheated at marbles. No other boys his age lived nearby. Scott's younger brother and sister played with each other, but he spent most the time by himself.

His secret hideaway was the *bushes*. It was in the back corner of their yard, an overgrown and abandoned orchard of apple trees and prickly plum bushes unattended for many years where no one else ever went. The bushes were nearly impassable because of the plum bushes that had sharp thorns. His father had cut a narrow path through the tangled thicket that led to an open space in the far end. An empty irrigation ditch came into the bushes from the property on the west side and ran along the north bordering the neighbor's fence. The irrigation ditch had once been fed with water from a dam on Beaver Creek, but was seldom used anymore and almost always empty. This was Scott's secret hiding place since no one else knew it was there. He liked to play war games along the ditch where he waged sea battles.

Other than those mornings last week when Rex was still at the Sewright's and he got to ride with Rex and Pop Bill to herd cattle to the pasture, the time waging sea battles in the empty irrigation ditch in the bushes was his favorite time of day.

Scott never told anyone about his war games; they might think they were silly and he'd be embarrassed – they wouldn't understand. Anyway, he liked them and there wasn't much else to do. He pretended the irrigation ditch was an ocean where he had landed his fleet of ships and established a naval base. The lids of old tin cans of different sizes and shapes became his ships -- battleships, aircraft carriers, and fast moving destroyers -- and he arranged his own fleet facing those of the enemy in huge sea battles up and down the empty ditch. He saved the best tin can lids for ships of his own fleet and misshapen ones became those of the enemy. Using his dad's pliers, he bent the ships of his fleet into shapes that reflected their armament. He dug a harbor along the side of the ditch where he could anchor his fleet and used rocks for docks.

Scott had a special feeling for the United States Navy since his older brother was sailor on anti-submarine duty in the North Atlantic.

All his ships had names. The battleships were named for states like in the U.S. Navy and he had the biggest battleships in the world in his fleet, just like in the real navy: the USS South Dakota, USS Iowa, USS Wisconsin, and the USS Missouri. Scott had three aircraft carriers which were named for battles: USS Coral Sea, USS Essex, and USS Enterprise. He had five cruisers and ten destroyers that are normally named for naval heroes, but he didn't give them names since they were only support ships for his battleships and aircraft carriers. Two of the battleships, one aircraft carrier, two cruisers and several destroyers were in task force #1 under the command of Admiral Halsey. Task force #2 with two battleships, one aircraft carrier, three cruisers and several destroyers were under Admiral Sprague. Scott pretended he was Admiral Nimitz and his headquarters was in a coffee can under a tree alongside the ditch. He never concerned himself with an anchorage for the enemy ships and they were left up and down the bank of the irrigation ditch depending on the status of a current battle.

Suddenly! An enemy fleet coming across the sea toward them had just been discovered by a PBY reconnaissance seaplane. Admiral Nimitz

BERNIE KEATING

28

ordered the task forces out-to-sea to face them in a defensive formation; so, he quickly positioned the battleships of Task Force #1 in a T formation with the destroyers out in front in a staggered shielding defensive line, and the aircraft carriers were kept in the rear of the task force where they were better protected, but their planes were still close enough that the torpedo planes could reach the enemy fleet and drop their missiles in the water aimed at the enemy aircraft carriers, and the dive bombers could dive straight down from five thousand feet and rain bombs on the enemy battleships below. Task Force #2 remained at sea further back in case they were needed. The battle was going well. It was awesome.

"Scott! Scott!! Come in," yelled his mother from the steps of the back porch. "It is time for canning. I need you. Come in now!!" Scott knew that sound; he had better head to the house; the sea battle would have to wait.

Almost every day during the summer there was canning: apples from the orchard, rhubarb given to them by a farmer friend, string beans and beets from their garden, and bushels and bushels full of tomatoes. He hated canning. His sister, Betty helped, but his little brother, Billy was too young. After his mother blanched the tomatoes so the skins would peal easily, his sister and he would complete the job and drop them into a pan where his mother would take over. The juice from the tomatoes left the skin on his hands pink and shriveled up. Mason jars covered all the kitchen counters most days, either in the process of being filled or cooling after his mother removed them from the pressure cooker. He never understood why it was necessary for him to always be there, since he really wasn't much help and only did the final part of the peeling job; but it seemed to be something she insisted on every day, like she didn't want to be in the kitchen alone by herself without her kids. Those canned tomatoes would be a vegetable for most evening meals during the winter when no fresh fruit or vegetables were available except for some things shipped in from else ware to the local stores that were very expensive. The family couldn't afford much of that store-bought food.

His dad raised a garden on the southern sunny side of the yard, and hoeing the garden was the other thing beside canning tomatoes that he got too much of. It was a boring chore. He'd go up and down the rows plunging his hoe about two inches into the dirt adjacent to the roots on each side of the tomato plants, peas, and string beans, just like his father instructed him to do; but he was never convinced it did any good, at least he couldn't see much change from day to day. His dad said it brought more oxygen to the roots and helped them grow better, but he found that hard to believe.

The town of Buffalo Gap now had public water. They drilled for water a year ago and pipes were laid through the town by men who worked on the WPA for the Federal Government. His family now had water that came to an outdoor faucet. Using a hose they could get enough water for the garden without relying on the irrigation ditch. The water pipes had not been extended inside their house with indoor plumbing, but they could at least get drinking water from the outdoor faucet next to the back porch and carry a bucket into the kitchen. The town water tasted a lot better than the rainwater they had to pump from the cistern under the back porch. Late in the summer as the rains tapered off, the cistern got close to empty and the taste got extremely bad. Another of his jobs was to keep the water bucket full and carry buckets of water from the outdoor faucet to the kitchen for doing dishes. The bucket sat on a stool in a corner of the kitchen with a dipper hanging on its side for the family to drink from, and it was his job to keep the bucket full with fresh water.

Some evenings during the summer, it would suddenly cloud up and Scott knew to get inside quickly because a lightning storm was about to hit. It was fun to sit in the dark with his family, hear the claps of thunder and watch the whole sky suddenly light up with the huge bolts of electricity. He didn't understand how thunder and lightning worked, but maybe someday when he grew up, he would. Then a sudden rainstorm would hit and he smelled the cool, fresh breeze that would make for good sleeping. Most likely Tomorrow would be just another boring day.

But, maybe tonight he could dream about something exciting and win another sea battle. He pulled the covers over his head and quickly fell asleep.

6

AN INDIAN WARDANCE
IN BUFFALO GAP!

The Fourth of July celebration in Buffalo Gap was epic; Scott couldn't wait for it to start and grew excited as the day approached. The celebration was a major event: fireworks, foot races, squaw wagon race down Main Street, water fight between firemen, rodeo, fireworks show from atop reservoir hill after dark, and a boot-stomping dance in the auditorium when Scott could stay up after midnight. People came to Buffalo Gap from all over and even from the Indian Reservation. Morning to night there was something sensational going on; it was amazing.

The celebration started the day before on July 3rd when a dozen wagons of Sioux Indians rolled into town from the Pine Ridge Indian Reservation twenty miles to the east. While the Fourth of July was a white man's celebration, it was also the occasion for a Sioux Indian celebration; but for a different reason. It was their opportunity to leave confinement on the Reservation and travel to Buffalo Gap where they could celebrate their heritage in the shadow of *pah-Ha SAH-pah*, their homeland. So while the townspeople of Buffalo Gap celebrated with games and fireworks, the Sioux Indians held ceremonies in a nostalgic return to their former way of life.

The Main Street of Buffalo Gap was the site of the Indian observance. Across the intersection from the bank were several vacant lots that extended to the south; this was the site of a tipi village that sprang up on

July 3rd. The Indians arrived in a caravan of horse-drawn wagons driven by squaws; with children hanging-on all over the wagons, and the procession was shepherded by two dozen warriors riding horses. The wagons arrived along the dirt road from the Indian Reservation, forded Beaver Creek just below the bridge, came across the railroad tracks, and proceeded west toward the bank. At the main intersection, the lead wagon turned into the vacant lots where the wagons formed a perimeter around a newly created village. Squaws erected a dozen tipis intermingled among the wagons, and horses were corralled in rope fences. The village came to life with a blaze under a tripod in front of each tipi. Indian families dwelled in a way of life much like that of their parents who lived here along Beaver Creek only a few decades before.

Scott stood with a crowd of townsfolk who gathered on the sidewalk in front of the bank and watched as the Indian wagons arrived and the new village was erected. The locals were fascinated with this colorful pageant that happened once a year; realizing this was a rare opportunity to see how the Indians had lived here in the cottonwood groves along Beaver Creek. Few people had much knowledge about the Indian culture.

"Good morning, Ed, quite a spectacle across the street," announced Charlie Streeter as he came to the bank corner and joined the large crowd."

"Sure is," responded John Degnan who had just come from his grocery store, leaving Nettie in charge. "Looks like they brought everything with them," he said with a laugh, "so I don't guess it will mean much business for Buffalo Gap.

"Look at those horses," voiced Frank Tower who owned several horses. "I'd like to have a couple of them like that buckskin mare with the white nose. Their wagons may be in bad shape, but they sure have a fine horse herd."

"Yeah," replied Degnan, "Wonder how they can live in such squalor as I hear they do out on the Reservation, yet afford such a great horse herd?"

"They inherited those horses from the frontier days," proclaimed Charlie Streeter, "and the horses came with them when they were forced to live on the Reservation. Some of those horses are probably decedents from the horses the explorer La Salle turned loose along the Mississippi River two hundred years ago. They've got some fine blood lines. " Charlie was one of the few in town who knew much about the Indians because several of them were his customers and rode saddles embossed with his emblem: *C.G. Streeter.*

"I suppose they will have their usual war dances tonight. Are you going to come watch them, Wes?

"Sure thing, I wouldn't miss it," responded Wes Dalbey. "We take these Sioux Indian ceremonies for granted, but this is one of the only places in the country where they are held; and I expect that someday they will become a passing craze just like Custer and his Seventh Cavalry have passed on into history."

"Wes, I think you are right. Well, anyway, I will be standing right here with you after dark watching them dance; and Wes, you bring Arloa and have her wear a long robe and she can go out with the squaws in the intersection and join in the dance. But, don't you try to join the warriors, I suggest you just stand here on the sidewalk and watch with me," declared Charlie as he chuckled; it was his big joke for the day, and he turned to walk back to his saddle shop to finish work on a saddle.

These Particular Indian families came from the Ogallala part of the reservation, well south of Cuny table where Scott's friend, Swallow, lived with his parents. His No-Water family living on Cuny Table owned a few head of cattle, a couple horses, did some farming, and lived in a frame house, all be it a meager and small hut. The mixed-blood Indians living on Cuny Table were considered by the Sioux living in the Oglala region of the Reservation as well-to-do. The full-blooded Sioux coming to Buffalo Gap for the celebration lived further south near the Indian Agency in great poverty and many lived in a tar-papered lean-to shack with a corrugated tin roof. They had not been assimilated into the ways of the white man, nor did they want to. Their parents had become forcefully confined by the U.S. Government on the reservation soon after the Battle of the Little Big Horn. While this next generation was now free to leave the reservation; where would they go, and what could they do? There was no place else where they would be welcome nor could earn a livelihood. While not openly hostile, they were ill-deposed; however, once a year they were welcomed into the little town of Buffalo Gap for these few short days in early July. In fact, they were urged to come since the Indian men, who were excellent riders, would be the principle bronco riders for the rodeo, and their wives would compete against each other in the squaw wagon race down the main street of Buffalo Gap. They were lured by the prospect of earning prize money sponsored by the tradespeople who owned the stores in town. The prize money earned by the Indians may be their only opportunity to see real cash during the year.

The night of July 3rd was Scott's favorite time. The Sioux men started a huge fire in the middle of the intersection in front of the bank. As darkness descended over the town, the sound of drums and chanting filled the air. The Indians left the Tipi village and poured into the intersection. A half dozen men pounded on leather drums, chanting a hypnotic beat, while warriors in full ceremonial dress with bow and arrow and spears cavorted and pranced around the fire in an unbroken circle. While the young men wore head bands and a single eagle feather, the elderly chiefs wore a full headdress with a long trace of eagle feathers trailing across their shoulders and tumbling down their backs. Across their chests were glittery beaded emblems hewn from porcupine quills and elk bones, woven together with leather thongs. Leggings were fashioned from deer hides and tied with leather straps; on their feet were moccasins crafted from buffalo hides.

This was their war-dance and they carried their weapons: spears, tomahawks, and bows with arrows in a pouch hanging from their shoulder; and they were ready for combat as they frolicked, pranced, and swaggered to the sound of the drum's rhythmic beat. Round and round they swayed as in a trance.

The Indian women, wearing deer hide robes that hung to the ground, were off to the side in a long line where they rocked and stepped in a heel-toe ballet to the beat of the drums.

Then the drum beats stopped momentarily; then began once again with a slower, sonorous, dirge-like sound, probably a funeral tale, and again later with an even stronger and faster beat as the warriors openly swaggered in an aggressive display of valor.

The ceremony began at dusk, and at ten o'clock it was still going strong. Scott's parents said it was time to go home. Tomorrow was the white man's 4th of July celebration. Scott couldn't wait for morning.

7

WAGONS ROARED DOWN MAIN STREET

Boom!! A blast was followed by a series of smaller explosions in rapid succession. Scott bounded out of bed. Oh my gosh! Wow! The 4th of July celebration had started. Rushing next door to the Streeter's, he saw Ed lighting some three pounders. They created a horrendous explosion. Then Ed started placing fire crackers under tin cans like rocket launchers and shooting them into the air. A couple coffee cans flew thirty feet into the air. Ed's dad, Charlie, got angry when a smoking tin can landed in the gutter on the Streeter porch.

"Damn it, Ed!" he shouted. "Do you want to start the house on fire? One more missile on the roof and it will be all over for you. Move out of the yard and into the street where it is safe before using any more firecrackers."

Scott was content to watch Ed Streeter shoot off his firecrackers, because he didn't have many of his own since his dad said they were too expensive. He wanted to save the few he had for later when he could shoot them off with his sparklers.

After breakfast he went down town and headed to Bert Doughty's barber shop where he knew the cowboys would be coming into town for their holiday shaves. By the time he got there, cowboys already occupied the chairs that were empty most days. Bert had few customers except for special days like the 4th of July, so he had space for only three patron chairs; but he did have an extra rotating barber chair next to the front window, a relic from years ago when he had a second barber working in his shop. Scott was usually able to sit in the front rotating chair that was always empty – Bert only did his work on the barber chair closest to the back window where a breeze from the back door kept the shop cooler. Today, the front barber chair was already occupied by a cowboy awaiting his turn for a shave. Scott stood leaning against the corner and watching the action. The cowboys were mostly interested in a shave since they preferred to keep their hair long where it could be tucked under their wide brimmed cowboy hats.

When their turn came, the cowboy sat down in the barber chair and Bert always started with a brief conversation to determine exactly how they wanted their shave performed. He listened carefully and may even ask some questions, although his routine never varied. He remembered only one way to do a shave, and it was the way he learned in barber school fifty years ago back in Indiana. He started by removing a steaming hot towel from the Bunsen-burner heated pot and dropping it on the customer's face to loosen up the whiskers. The startled cowboy flinched, not expecting anything so hot. The towel was left on the face for a couple minutes loosening up whiskers; during which time Bert made small talk to put the cowboy at ease, while also slashing his shaving knife up and down a leather strap hanging on the barber chair to hone the edge of the blade to razor thin. Then he removed the wet towel and peered closely at the cowboy's face to determine exactly where to start the shave and how it should be accomplished. This was more than a token glance because Bert was nearly blind and had to get close to focus clearly.

For a cowboy, this shave in the Buffalo Gap barber shop was like a celebration in itself. They hated to shave in the ranch bunkhouse with cold water in a basin followed by an evening with nothing to do in the isolation of a ranch many miles from town. There was no social action at the ranch. The shave by Bert got them prepared for Buffalo Gap's big events: celebration on Main Street, afternoon rodeo, and the dance in the evening. There would be cowgirls at the dance and cowboys wanted to look their best. They rode to town with a decorated, brightly colored dress shirt in the pack behind their saddle they were saving for the dance in the evening.

Blutch Wilson, Gus Haaser, and a couple other cowboys wore side arms, colts tied down in a holster. They always wore them on the open range, but on this occasion in town it was mostly for show. Carrying a gun was not a big thing for them because they normally rode on the open range with a side arm or a rifle in the boot to use against prey such as coyotes or cougars. They also used them to kill the rattlesnakes that were constantly spooking their horses, causing them sometimes to get bucked off.

Scott leaned against the corner by the door with wide-open eyes and took it all in. He knew the cowboys and ranchers by name because he heard his father and mother talking about them, and most of them knew he was the banker's kid. They were all customers of his dad at the bank, but this was the only time he got to see them up close and sitting down. They usually rode their horses to town and tied the reins to the hitching post in front of the bank where he could watch them striding into the bank as he sat on the sidewalk in the shade.

"Ain't you the Keating kid, the banker's son," asked Blutch Wilson when he enter the shop and sat in the front barber chair to wait his turn.

"Yes sir, I am," Scott responded rather tentatively because Blutch Wilson wore side arms and had a reputation as one of the meanest cowboys on the open range. His father and an older brother were prominent ranchers and friends of Scott's dad at the bank, but Blutch was a hell-raising maverick who worked odd jobs for other ranchers who would tolerate his bad behavior since he was known as the best all-around working cowboy on the open range. He could live with only a bed role and frying pan for weeks at a time, summer and winter in the rugged badlands and keep a rancher's herd together and safe from all the predators. There were few others who matched his cowboy abilities, but no one matched his meanness when he came to town, threw down a few whiskeys, got drunk, and challenged all comers to a fight. Frenchie's saloon was his place of work in town.

"Well, Kid, I'm going to be riding this afternoon at the rodeo," Blutch said in a friendly sounding voice. "Are you going – you'd better be?"

"Yes sir," Scott responded meekly. He didn't want any trouble for his dad with Blutch Wilson.

"Good. Keep an eye out for me because I'm going to ride the wildest and highest bronco out of chute number one, and when I come out of the chute I'll give you a wave," he said it while laughing. Scott smiled too, but he knew this was a joke since all riders of broncos had to keep one hand raised high as they exited the chute.

"Blutch, you're next," announced Bert. Even thought it was not really Blutch's turn yet, Bert did not want any trouble with him and the other customer's would understand or at least not challenge Bert's moving him ahead in the queue. Everyone in town was intimidated by this ornery and unpredictable cowboy. Give him a shave and get him out the shop as quickly as possible!

"Do you want your usual shave, Blutch?"

"Yeah, Bert, and make it extra special. I might get me a date with the prettiest cowgirl on the range tonight, even though she doesn't know it yet." Then he laughed, and Bert smiled as he dropped the steaming hot towel on Blutch's face.

By mid-morning it was time for the races along Main Street and Scott sat on the sidewalk waiting for the action to start. Wes Dalbey was the man in charge. He ran most activities in town, including appointing himself as the umpire of the weekly softball game on the diamond east of the railroad tracks. While Wes was raised from childhood in Buffalo Gap, he never had to make a living in town, so was considered by everyone as completely impartial. While still a teenager he went to work as a maintenance worker on the railroad section crew. He became a union official after many years and was elected the secretary-treasurer for the Maintenance-of-Way Union for the Chicago Northwestern railroad area north of Omaha. He was an official and could locate his office anywhere he wanted it on the railroad line between Omaha, Nebraska and Sheridan, Wyoming; so, he decided to locate it in his hometown of Buffalo Gap where his mother, Grandma Dalbey, still lived. His wife, Arlo, was his secretary. So the Dalbeys were special in town because they were financially insulated from the hardship of the depression and not dependent on anything or anyone local. Wes also had plenty of time to organize local events, so he did most of them, and the town was happy to oblige and let him do it.

Scott ran in the under-12 race that started in front of Frenchies saloon with the finish line a block down the street in front of the bank where the judges Fred Degnan and Ira Thurston were standing. Wes Dalbey raised his pistol in the air and fired the starting shot. Scott got a poor start but ran as fast as he could. He got only a second place, but he earned a bag of tootsie rolls anyway, compliments of the Tower Grocery store. His mother ran with all the other ladies in the Married Ladies race, but it ended in disaster for her when she tripped and ended up falling in the dirt and skinning her knee. All the men standing on the sidewalk got a big kick out of seeing her fall down, she being the banker's wife.

Just at that moment, the Norman pickup came down the street, parked in front of the Tower grocery store, and Rex jumped over the tailgate out of the back where he had been riding and came running down the sidewalk. Scott was glad to see his friend who would give him someone to talk to.

"Hi, Rex."

"Hello, Scott."

"You should've seen my mother's race. She was coming in first until she stumbled and fell down. I ran in a race but got a bad start and lost to Billy Bain, who is always jumping the gun and cheating. Anyway, I got a bag of candy. Do you want one of my tootsie rolls, they're pretty good," he said as he reached out with a tootsie roll.

"I guess. I don't like them much because they're always getting stuck in my teeth and are hard to chew", he responded as he took the piece of candy from Scott's outstretched hand.

"Rex, you're just in time. The three-legged race is about to start, and you can enter with me and we can be partners."

"Great. What is the three-legged race like?"

"Our two inside legs get tied together, so we have to run together as a team and keep in step or else we'll stumble."

"Okay, sounds okay to me. How do we keep in step with each other?"

"I guess we'll have to count with each other, left, right, left, right, so we keep in time. I'll be doing the counting out loud"

"That won't work. We can't both be on the left foot at the same time because my left foot will be tied with your right foot."

"Oh, that's right. I know, I'll say middle, and we both know to put our weight on the middle leg, and then we can both use our outside foot next. Let's use my belt and tie our legs and practice."

"Sure. I hope your pants don't fall down without a belt. But maybe all the other guys would laugh so hard they'd stop running and we could win."

"Good idea. Just when Wes Dalbey shoots the pistol to start the race, I'll drop my pants."

After a couple minutes of practice with their center legs strapped together, and falling a couple times in the process, they learned how to run together with Rex in charge.

"Scott, I'll do the counting and you follow me," Rex announced with authority. He was used to taking charge and speaking brazenly this way to the hired hand, Mike, back at the ranch.

Scott and Rex took first place in the three legged race and beat Billy Bain and Daryl Thompson. The potato sack race came next in which they had to step inside a gunny sack so it was like their two legs were tied together. The sack came up to their waist and they had to hold the top with their two hands as they hopped forward. It required good balance or they could fall headlong into the dirt. For some reason, Rex did not want to enter and stood on the sidewalk to watch the race. Scott was ready for the starting gun this time, and he led the race from the start. He got a bag of lollypops for first place from the Phillips grocery store and gave one to Rex.

Under the supervision of Wes Dalbey and Ira Thurston, the street was cleared of all pedestrians who had to move up onto the sidewalk. Even the cars parked on Main Street in front of Myme's Inn had to be moved before the Squaw Wagon Race could begin. The street must be completely cleared so all the wagons had the opportunity to pass each other. The race could be dangerous. Three wagons pulled by teams of horses were driven from the Indian Tipi village and lined up in the intersection in front of the bank. Sitting on the front driver bench of each wagon was an Indian lady holding the reins of the team of horses, and alongside was a second squaw holding the braking lever and a whip. Wes Dalbey in his most distinguished manner stood beside the starting line with a raised pistol. With a shot, they were off. The wagons roared down Main Street in a cloud of dust as the squaws flogged their horses with whips to urge them faster. They raced neck-and-neck past Frenchie's saloon into the second block past Charlie Streeter's Saddle Shop, where the race ended. ...

It took another half block for the team of horses to be braked to a stop. The ladies turned the three wagons around in the street one at a time and slowly returned to the starting line at the bank intersection. Wes Dalbey approached the winning wagon and with considerable fanfare awarded the winning team four ten-dollar bills, which was a lot of money for a race. It was by far the biggest prize awarded. Then he gave the drivers of the other two wagons each two ten-dollar bills. They stuffed the bills in their pockets and drove the teams of horses pulling the wagons into the tipi village. That was the last race of the morning.

Then everyone walked two blocks down the street behind the bank in the direction of school house where the water fight was to be held in a vacant lot. All the participants were members of the local Volunteer Fire Department, the largest organization in town and an extremely important one because the surrounding range lands were so vulnerable to fire, particularly those started by lightning or from the exhaust of tractors when harvesting hay. The prosperity of the town would become jeopardized with a range fire. There were two teams composed of businessmen, ranchers, and cowboys, all members of the Volunteer Fire Department. Most of the men were under forty years of age, the water fight being too rough for the elderly. The postmaster, Jack Nolan, and his brother Jim, who worked at his dad's grain elevator, were the two team captains.

A coin was flipped by Ira Thurston and Jim Nolan won the toss so got to choose his first team member. Then the captains took turns calling out names until each team had a dozen members. Ira Thurston, Captain of the Fire Department, was the referee. He stood at a finish line where a rope lying on the ground marked the center line between the opponents. The two teams lined up and lifted up the fire hose spigots, hanging on tightly to the fire hoses that were under extreme water pressure. The teams were separated by a distance of fifteen feet between them. The team captains flipped open the hose spigot and a powerful stream of water shot out of the hoses up in the air, much like crossed swords at the beginning of a duel. Ira Thurston raised a pistol and shot into the air and the contest started.

Jack Nolan, who was the in lead position of his team holding the spigot, pointed his hose directly at his brother's team, and Jim Nolan was nearly knocked off his feet by the blast of water. He retaliated, taking dead aim at Jack. Everyone became drenched, including nearby spectators. The teams fought back and forth with the powerful streams of water that shot out the end of the hoses with enough force to reach the top of a five-story building, four stories higher than any building in town except for Myme's Inn. Several men were knocked off their feet and staggered away, only to return again to their position along the fire hose in a display of bravo. The contest was ended when Jack Nolan's team forced the other to retreat back beyond the rope finish line.

Scott loved watching the fire hose fight -- it was awesome. What could be more fun than watching all the men in town getting beat-up and knocked off their feet by the blasts of water. The spectators were mostly children since all the men were on the teams; few women showed up for the event, there being no place for them to safely stand without getting soaked. When it was all over, the entire vacant lot was a pool of mud and Scott was drenched.

It was time for lunch and Scott went home to get into some dry clothes for a hot dog. They had to leave early for the rodeo since his dad was the Treasurer who handed all the prize money for the winning bronco riders. His dad's station was on a raised platform over the chutes where the rodeo judges and an announcer were positioned. There was one judge who was the timer and two in the arena standing next to the chute gates where they could witness the ride of the cowboy. They had to judge both the horse and the cowboy: did the cowboy dug his spurs hard enough into the shoulder of the horse when exiting the chute, was the horse a sufficiently wild bucking bronco, and did the cowboy give a good ride without grabbing for leather before the time was up? Gus Haaser, a rancher who rode broncos when he was young, was one of the gate judges in the arena. The other was Charles Cuny from the reservation, a mixed-blood Indian whose word was gospel with all the Indian bronco riders. Elmer Elton was the timer judge on the platform. The judges were all cowboys from birth and highly respected by all the locals. Their decisions were considered final. At the conclusion of each event, it was Scott's dad, Frank McCormick, who handed the prize money to the cowboys.

Saddle bronco riding was the opening event and out of chute number one on a black stallion was Francis Stands-alone. He was an Indian who lived with his family in an abandoned rail boxcar on a vacant lot a next to the Sewright ranch. Francis worked for Sewright full time during the summer except when he was riding in rodeos. He was always friendly with Scott. There were a number of things required in a saddle riding contest: the cowboy had to dig his spurs into the front shoulder of the bronco when exiting the chute to create instant bucking, he had to keep his right arm raised above his head, and he had to stay on the horse for eight seconds. Any time before the eight seconds are up, if the cowboy grabbed for the saddle horn to stay on the horse or is thrown from the horse, he is automatically disqualified. Unfortunately for Francis, the black stallion was a particularly wild horse that circled like a corkscrew round-and-round and Francis was thrown from the saddle before the time was up and he landed on his butt in a cloud of dust.

Scott and Rex sat with their mothers in the grandstand bleachers where they watched the rodeo events. The bleachers had a dozen rows of planks and all spaces were filled with spectators. Crude outhouse toilets were located a hundred feet in the field behind the bleachers. Scott tapped Rex on the shoulder as a signal, and they left their mothers in the bleachers as if the boys were headed to the outhouse toilet, but they circled around behind the bleachers and snuck over to the rodeo corrals where they climbed up onto the top rail of the rodeo fences adjacent to the chutes. Kids were not supposed to be in the corral area, but because his dad was an official in the platform over the chutes, Scott was sure he could get away with it and not be chased back to the grandstands. Sitting on the top rail and watching the action close up, they considered themselves as cowboys. From this vantage position sitting close to the chutes, they were able to watch as rodeo workers in the corrals behind the chutes manhandled the wild broncos to get them in place and saddled for a ride. As each horse entered the chute, other cowboys placed a saddle on the bronco and carefully cinched-up the saddle by reaching with prongs through the planks of the chutes. It was dangerous work, but they had done it many times before and knew what they were doing. Watching the rodeo helpers in the back corrals was a lot more interesting than sitting with all those other people and their mothers in the bleachers. And sitting on the top rail with his saddle pal Rex Norman, who was a real cowboy from a ranch, gave Scott a special feeling. Blutch Wilson had a conspicuous presence at the rodeo. In addition to riding a bronco, he and his brother, Frank, were the two pickup men. They were chosen because they were recognized as the top cowboy riders, and a pickup man requires the skill of a top hand. They have to be strong and able to manhandle a wild bucking bronco while protecting the cowboy from injury. It was their job to assist the cowboy and keep him safe from the wild horse once they exited the chute or if they were bucked-off. If the rider was thrown off, the pickup man would position himself between the bronco and the man lying on the ground. If a cowboy was successful in staying on for the required eight seconds, then it was the job of the pickup man to get him safely off the bronco. Here the two pickup men worked together as a team. One would ride to the left side of the bucking horse, grab the halter rope and snug it around his saddle horn, pulling the bronco up against his own horse. The other pickup man would ride to the right side, reach across to grab the saddle horn on the bronco and present a target for the cowboy to grab ahold of so he could swing over the back of the pickup man and fall safely onto the ground. All this action takes place at top speed with a wild, bucking bronco. It requires the ultimate in cowboy skill.

After the saddle bronco riding, next came the steer dogging contest. A steer would be sent at full speed out of a chute; two cowboys would ride from behind on either side of the steer, with the job to tackle the steer. The purpose of the cowboy on the right was to push up against the steer and keep it running close to the cowboy riding on the other side. When nearly alongside the steer, the cowboy on the left would reach down grabbing the horns of the steer and leap from his own saddle onto the side of the steer, digging his heels into the ground in an attempt to stop the steer. As they came to a stop, he placed his arms around the horns and violently twisted the head so the steer would fall on its side onto the ground. It was an ultimate display of strength, horsemanship, bravo, and skill. In a previous year, Blutch Wilson had set a local record time of six seconds from the time the steer exited the chute until it was on its side. This year there were five in the steer dogging contest, and all of them were Indian riders from the Reservation. Scott watched as George High-Eagle won the event in ten seconds.

Scott and Rex returned to the bleachers from the direction of the outhouses so their mothers would not know they had gone to the chute area. Children were forbidden to go to the horse corrals since it was such a dangerous area. The mothers said nothing, so the boys may have got away with their mischief. When the rodeo was over, Scott and his mother returned home for supper.

Shortly after supper, they watched the fireworks display that was shot-off from atop Reservoir Hill. Later in the evening was the big 4th of July dance in the auditorium sponsored by the Volunteer Fire Department. The dance never started until after nine o'clock.

Scott never understood why adults loved to go to a dance, because he found it rather boring, except when he and Rex explored in the dark outside of the auditorium among the parked cars that extended on all sides and down the street. He loved exploring in the dark when he had the security of someone else with him. It was an adventure even though it was scary, but it was more fun and not so scary with Rex alongside.

Once the dance music started, the two boys headed outside. There wasn't much to see early in the evening because some people were still arriving and parking their cars, but later on it became more fun. They were able to spy looking through the back windows on some couples who were kissing and hugging each other. It was so funny. There were whiskey bottles everywhere and sometimes they found dollar bills that had been dropped on the ground.

The Buffalo Gap auditorium was sixty years old but still used for every event in town because there was no other place big enough for a crowd. Scott had performed on the stage in the Auditorium when he was in the fourth grade for a school play, Charles Dickens's *Christmas Carol* that Miss Hazek put on with a cast of all the kids in school. The auditorium was also used during the winter for basketball games. A raised stage was on one end and narrow balconies ran the length of the other three sides facing the stage. Stairs led up to the balconies and a small kitchen area. The local ladies used this upstairs kitchen to prepare sandwiches to be served at midnight, a tradition for all the dances. After the light meal, the dancing would start again until the wee hours. Scott loved to spend time on the balcony because it led to the back of the stage and onto the balcony on the other side. From his time performing in the school play, he knew his way around back stage, and he led Rex behind the front curtain and showed him the darkened dressing rooms.

The dances in Buffalo Gap never started before nine o'clock when everyone in town had finished their supper and the ladies had redone their rodeo makeup and were dressed with the special clothes they saved for the dance. The dance was always a dressy affair. The ladies wore their best and fanciest dresses and the men wore business suits and ties. Even the ranchers wore embroidered long-sleeved shirts, vests, and bolo ties, and the cowboys wore their brightest shirts with embroidered emblems on the sleeves and a bright neckerchief around the neck.

Before the dancing started, Wes Dalbey, who was the dance chairman, slowly circled the floor sprinkling flaks from an Ivory soap box onto the floor to make it slick enough for dancing. Scott's dad opened up the ticket window in the front doorway where he sold tickets to everyone who entered. John Degnan collected the tickets and used an ink pad to stamp wrists so everyone could come and go during the intermissions. The 4th of July dance was a fund raising event in support of the Volunteer Fire Department. Scott's dad was also treasurer of the organization, a job he inherited as the banker because he was the only one the local people trusted with money. There were only three dances held in the auditorium during the year: the New Year's Eve dance, the Catholic Ladies Saint Patrick's dance, and the 4th of July dance, and Scott's dad was the ticket seller for all three. Since he did not enjoy dancing, he was satisfied to spend his time in the ticket booth and visit with the incoming people, all of whom were customers of his at the bank.

The music started slowly as the musicians warmed up. The local band had been organized by Ira Thurston and he was the band leader who picked the music and started all the numbers. In his youth he had taken trumpet lessons from a neighbor and loved music. As the other musicians warmed up, Ira sat quietly holding his trumpet because when he raised it to his lips it would be a cue for the band to start playing the opening song. Ira was a mechanic in his dad's garage and also ran the road grader for the roads south of town. His dad, Floyd Thurston, worked part-time for the county as the road maintenance grader and he maintained the important gravel roads like highway #79 between Buffalo Gap and Hot Springs while his son, Ira, did the dirt roads. In addition to running the Thurston garage, they were hired by the county to keep the roads in passable shape. Whenever the dirt roads became deeply rutted after heavy rains or the gravel was piled up too high along the shoulders, the locals were quick to express their displeasure to Floyd and Ira. The condition of the roads was important to everyone in town because the roads were their only link to the outside world. Even at their best, the dirt and gravel roads were marginal and uncomfortable to travel.

Leo Mohler, a rancher from Harrison Flat who played the guitar, was the first to start tuning-up as he lightly strummed his strings, made adjustments with the pegs, and gradually became satisfied with the sound. Dale Lovell, who was Scott's teacher in the fifth grade, played the trombone. It was an instrument he mastered when he was in high school where he was raised in the eastern part of the state. Since the band featured several Glenn Miller arrangements, the trombone was an important instrument in the band; Dale played it with finesse as he moved the slide in and out with much flourish. Dorothy Harmon played the piano. She was the only member of the band who could sight read music with any skill and the only one with a sheet of the music in front of her. All the rest played by ear or memory. Leo Mohler's seventy-five year old father, Hilmer, played the fiddle, an instrument he learned as a youngster from his own father back in Kentucky. Jack Nolan, the postmaster, was on the drums. He'd never had any musical training, but his job was only to keep the beat by pounding his foot on the pedal of the base drum with an occasional flourish on the snare drums.

Ira Thurston lifted his trumpet to his lips and the band music started. For their opening song they had rehearsed one of the currently popular Glenn Miller songs, *String of Pearls*, and the band started off with all musicians playing in the same key. While none of them were professionals and seldom played together except for a dance, they managed to make good music. What they lacked in sophistication, they made up for with volume. Jack Nolan kept a good beat on the drums for the dancers, but the band only occasionally meshed with all the instruments in perfect pitch; but each song ended in a flourish with a final cord that found all of them in tune and giving the final note a full blast. Adding to the music was the rhythm of cowboys stomping their high heel boots on the dance floor that vibrated up and down with the song; the auditorium was filled with ear-splitting musical sounds.

While Scott's dad was busy most the night selling tickets in the booth, his mother was asked for nearly every dance by one of the ranchers or cowboys. They all knew her from the bank, where she often worked part time to help her husband, and it seemed almost an obligation for them to dance with the banker's wife. She didn't mind since she loved to dance and knew all the men by first and last name, and also the status of their bank account, mortgage, or collateral on their cattle herds. It was a small town and important for her to make a good impression with all the townspeople and ranchers at the dance who were customers at the bank.

During intermissions all the men left the auditorium to go outside and join each other in small groups around their cars. This was a social event where friendships were nurtured and business often transacted. The host rancher of each small group would open the car door, reach inside the front compartment for his bottle of whiskey and pass it around. Each man would raise the bottle in a salute to the host, wipe the top of the bottle with his sleeve, take a sip, and pass the bottle to another. The bottle would go around the circle, ending with the host who took the final sip and returned it to the front compartment. Ranchers were interested to learn who had hay for sale, where they could locate a good bull, and if anyone was thinking of selling a pasture or placing one out for lease. A lot of business was transacted informally during the visit. At each intermission, Scott's dad was with a different group of ranchers and all of them were interested in talking business matters with him.

The ladies stayed in the auditorium during the intermission and sat visiting with each other on the chairs that lined the perimeter of the dance floor, or went to the upstairs kitchen to start preparing sandwiches for the midnight snack.

As the evening progressed, Wes Bondurant a rancher from the Cheyenne River country would organize a square dance. There were normally about six squares and each consisted of four couples, so it took some time for Bondurant to get things organized. When the fiddle music started, the dancers would go through the sequence of promenades, allemande-lefts, side-steps, and the other square dance routines all the dancers were familiar with. The music always started with a lively rendition of *Turkey in the Straw* with Hilmer Mohler featured on the fiddle and his son, Leo, on the guitar.

Scott and Rex grew tired of playing outside in the dark and came inside, climbing the stairs up to the balcony where they leaned on the railing and watched the dancers below. The balcony was somewhat of a babysitting operation with two ladies who kept a watchful eye on numerous children who had been left there. No one in Buffalo Gap used a babysitter for a dance since they all brought their children; it was a social event for the entire family. The young girls often danced with each other, but boys seldom danced with girls until they were in high school. Scott and Rex thought dancing was silly or were shy around girls and content to watch from the balcony.

Suddenly there was a commotion on the dance floor when Blutch Wilson rode his horse through the front door, past Scott's dad at the ticket booth, and onto the dance floor among the dancers. Blutch was very drunk. As he rode to the middle of the dance floor, he pulled a pistol from his holster and, keeping time with the music, began shooting into the air and yelling at the top of his voice. Scott and Rex looked down from the balcony, and then sprang back to the wall to avoid being hit by bullets that whistled past them to the ceiling. Wes Dalbey and Frank McCormick rushed onto the dance floor to intercept the drunken cowboy on his horse. Scott's dad grabbed the reins while Wes Dalbey and several ranchers assisted Blutch off the horse where he fell to the floor in a drunken stupor. The horse was led out the front door and tied to the front bumper of a nearby car. Some ranchers dragged Blutch out through the front door across the porch and let him fall onto the ground in the dark. The band scarcely missed a beat and the music continued. Everyone knew Blutch Wilson and had seen his kind of drunken behavior before. Scott's mother came to the balcony, got Scott, and together they left; it already was an hour past midnight.

Scott crawled into bed. Wow! That was the best 4th of July ever. It was Epic!

8

BACKSEAT IN A 'MODEL A' FORD

It was Sunday: Frank McCormick's one day from work. With no vacations in ten years, he worked six days every week. As the manager of the Buffalo Gap State Bank with no back-up except for his wife, who filled in when he was occasionally too ill to open the doors of the bank, Frank was the only man with the combination to the vault's outside steel door and the safe inside the vault that held all the money. He ran the bank; hence, the heart of business in Buffalo Gap and the surrounding ranch lands.

Frank worked six days a week from seven when he arrived until evening when the doors were closed to customers and he started to do the posting of the day's activities into ledger accounts. He accepted deposits, cashed checks, made loans, collected payments, sold insurance, and visited the ranches of those in default to negotiate partial payments and help them avoid foreclosure.

On Sunday after attending church services with the family, his day of relaxation involved three priorities depending on the season: a family picnic in the Black Hills; trout fishing on Beaver Creek; and driving his 1932 Model A Ford with his family to Hot Springs to see a movie. His favorite actors were Nelson Eddy and Jeanette MacDonald. Today the family was headed to Hot Springs to see the movie *Indian Love Call* starring his favorite couple.

The Model A Ford was the state-of-the-art automobile for that era. It was later inventions that came with car radio, air-conditioning, and seat belts that started American family life down the road to oblivion. Until then, a car ride was a shared family togetherness. Dad sang with gusto as he steered the Model A Ford down the gravel road, wind blowing in through the open windows

> *With someone like you,*
> *A pal so good and true,*
> *I'd like to leave it all behind*
> *And go and find*

Denis sat in the middle of the front seat between Mother and Dad. In the backseat, Scott and his sister, Betty, and two brothers, Edwin and Billy, shared the crowded backseat and two open windows with wind in their face.

> *A place that's known to God alone*
> *Just a spot we could call our own*
> *We'll find perfect peace where joys never cease*
> *Somewhere beneath the starry skies.*

> *We'll build …*

"Scott, stop bothering Billy and behave yourself," scolded
Mother without even looking over her shoulder. How did she know Scott was taunting his little brother because he wanted Billy's place next to the open window … "and Edwin, you're not too old to sing with the rest of us. Now behave yourself and sing."

It was a Sunday afternoon drive to Hot Springs to see the first movie for the summer. There were no movies in Buffalo Gap, except for those in the Grange Hall when the soap salesman came to town and showed horse-racing movies projected against a sheet hanging on a wall; but those movies weren't that great because he kept interrupting them with commercials to sell his soap.

But this afternoon the family was headed to a real movie in a real theatre and the stars were Frank McCormick's favorites, Nelson Eddy and Jeanette MacDonald in their 1936 hit, *Indian Love Call.* … And if Betty didn't get carsick and delay them, the family would be early enough to get the best seats in the front row. It promised to be an amazing afternoon.

We'll build a sweet little nest
Somewhere out in the west
And let the rest of the world go by.

A car came down the road. "Here comes a car. Quick, roll up the windows!" shouted Dad as he interrupted the song. The dirt road stirred up a cloud of dust, and rolling up the windows was a small price to pay for clean air, and then down again to let it back in.

It was a great movie. On the ride back home to Buffalo Gap, Scott fell asleep curled up in the back seat. He dreamt of wearing the bright red coat of the Canadian Mounted Police, like Nelson Eddie. With his rich baritone, he was singing to Jeanette MacDonald, and echoes of the song were reverberating off the mountain peaks

When I'm calling you - Oo Oo Oo
Will you answer too - Oo Oo Oo
That means I offer my love to you
To be your own. ...

Perhaps the words were not the same since Scott couldn't remember them exactly from the movie; but no matter, Jeanette was listening and smiling at him. He heard her beautiful soprano response his song.

You belong to me,
I'll belong to you.

Back home that night for supper sitting next to his Dad, they ate his favorite Sunday bedtime snack, a big bowl of soda crackers and ice cold milk. With a new electric refrigerator, they always had milk that was fresh and cold – not like last year when all they had was an ice box and warm milk. He had a second bowl; then went to bed, and dreamed about Jeanette. Those were sweet dreams.

CAVALRY TROOPERS RIDING
UP SCHOOL HILL

Two hundred and sixty eight troopers killed. June 16, 1876: Scott could tell you what that date meant; it was when General Custer and five companies of the Seventh Cavalry were wiped-out at the Battle of the Little Big Horn. Scott knew everything about the battle: he had read every book and seen movies.

Swallow's grandfather, No-Water, could also tell you about that day; he was there. As a teenage warrior in Chief Sitting Bull's tribe of Sioux, he remembered the day that changed his life. Cavalry troops charged into their tipi village along the river they called Greasy Grass and slaughtered women and children. Scattering in the aftermath of the battle, his tribe had fled north into Canada; later to be herded like cattle onto the Pine Ridge Indian Reservation and forced to live confined in the misery of Reservation life. He had spent the fifty years since then hating the U.S. Cavalry.

After the battle, the remnants of the Seventh Cavalry were relocated to Fort Meade, an army post at the northern edge of the Black Hills seventy miles north of Buffalo Gap. As the frontier gradually became settled by white pioneers with the Indians no longer a threat, the cavalry engaged in mock war games and ceremonial duties. It is difficult to understand why a regiment that decisively lost its last battle should be so highly honored by the United States; nevertheless, the Seventh Cavalry became legendary and its troopers honored as heroes. At least Scott and all the white people considered them that way: it is doubtful that No-Water or his grandson, Swallow, felt the same.

During the decade of the nineteen thirties, the Seventh Cavalry at Fort Meade was the last contingent of horse cavalry in the United States Army. Each spring the regiment made a week-long march from Fort Meade passing through Buffalo Gap on the way to Fort Robinson in Nebraska. It was a two hundred mile march taking ten days. They rode twenty miles every day and bivouacked each night. Buffalo Gap was one of their stopping places. The large open space behind the school, which was used as a playground during Scott's recesses and as a softball field, became a 7th cavalry bivouac for the night

The people of Buffalo Gap were thrilled to watch the famous regiment riding their horses four abreast along Main Street and up School House Hill to their bivouac in the field behind. While the cavalry normally wore khaki when at Fort Meade, for this annual event all the troopers were dressed-up wearing the cavalry blue and officers with swords, seen only in Hollywood movies. Scott had seen the movie "*They Died with Their Boots On*" starring Errol Flynn when his parents took him to the movie theatre in Hot Springs. It was a movie about the Seventh Cavalry when General Custer and his men had all been killed at the Battle of the Little Big Horn and Errol Flynn had the role of General Custer who was the last to die.

In June, school was out for the summer and Swallow was again living with his family at the No-Water encampment on the Sewright ranch on Beaver Creek; Scott and Swallow were waiting at the bottom of School House Hill for the arrival of the Seventh Cavalry. Scott was so excited he could hardly wait for their arrival. Swallow had been playing with him when it became time to walk to School House Hill; so he accompanied Scott, but the arrival of the cavalry meant little to him. There was no celebration by Indians to honor the unit that had killed so many of their ancestors.

"Here they come," shouted Scott.

Leading the contingent was a tall heavily decorated colonel carrying a sword just like General Custer and dressed in the cavalry blue Scott had seen in movies. He rode a white stallion, the tallest horse Scott had ever seen. Riding with a ram-rod back in a rolling cadence with his horse, he looked neither to left or right.

"Yeah, Colonel!" yelled Scott at the top of his voice. The regiment commander looked over in his direction, saw Scott, smiled, and lifted his hand from the saddle horn, the traditional greeting from one cavalry man to another. Scott was proud; the colonel of the 7th cavalry had given him a salute. It was epic.

Behind the Colonel rode the color guard: a bugler and two troopers carrying the U.S. flag and 7th Cavalry emblem. As a Boy Scout, Scott knew the etiquette so he stood at attention and saluted the flag as it passed in review. Swallow stood alongside and wondered what the fuss was all about, the flag meant nothing to his people on the Indian Reservation.

Behind the colors came the fifty troopers of Company A. At their head rode a captain on a coal-black stallion that was at least seventeen hands high, which Scott knew was how cowboys measured the height of a horse. Pop Bill's horse, Whitey, was sixteen hands high. Every trooper of Company A rode a coal-black steed. Each had rolled-up packs behind their saddle and a rifle in the boot hanging from the saddle. They were the first of six companies of the Seventh Cavalry that passed in front of Scott and Swallow. The three-hundred troopers advanced up School House Hill to their bivouac behind the school.

"Yeah Captain!" Scott yelled to the leader out in front of Company A. The captain looked over at him, smiled, and lifted his hand in a salute. Scott was thrilled. He had been saluted by a captain of the Seventh Cavalry.

"Wow! Did you see that Swallow?" We were saluted by the captain."

"What does salute mean?" Swallow queried somewhat puzzled.

"It is a way of saying hello and paying respect. In the Boy Scouts we salute the flag by giving a salute at the beginning of every meeting when we say the Pledge of Allegiance. We show our respect."

"On the reservation we don't salute the cavalry."

"I can understand that. The Seventh Cavalry fought against your Grandfather when he was a warrior fighting against them, but it was a long time ago, Swallow, so you and I don't have anything to do with that." Scott understood that Swallow would have a different outlook on the cavalry troopers riding in front of them. In a sense, the troopers represented the enemy of his Indian people. He understood it, but that was all in the past and a long time ago as far as he was concerned. A lot of Indians had been killed by the cavalry, so Scott didn't think the battle or movie about General Custer was good to discuss with Swallow. But Scott loved the Seventh Cavalry, their beautiful horses and the troopers who wore their blue uniforms with all their belongings in a pack behind the saddle, and a rifle in the boot hanging alongside the stirrup.

"Wow!" Scott exclaimed, "The famous Black Horse Company is coming up the hill. They're extremely famous. Look at those horses; they're the biggest and best I've ever seen. Oh my gosh! Epic!"

On-and-on the cavalry troops came – three hundred. There were six companies, fifty mounted troopers in each, and all the horses in each company were the same color: Company A horses were all coal-black; Company B horses all bays; Company C all sorrels; Company D horses were blood bays; Company E all grays; Company F had horses of mixed colors; and the color guard rode white stallions just like the Colonel. Scott's favorite was Company A leading the regiment on their beautiful coal-black steeds.

"Come on, Swallow, we can't follow them up the hill, but we can sneak around the school and climb the fire guard exit on the back of the school and watch them set up camp." As the last ranks of the Regiment passed, the two boys rushed up the path to the school and circled around to the back where they positioned themselves on the fire guard balcony.

After the troopers had watered, rubbed down, and picketed their horses, they pitched their tents in long rows and completed setting up camp. Then townspeople were then permitted to enter. Scott and Swallow were the first into the cavalry camp. It did not occur to Scott at the time that this was the same U.S. Cavalry regiment that Swallow's grandfather, no-Water, had defeated at the Battle of the Little Bighorn and later was involved in the Massacre of Wounded Knee on the Pine Ridge Indian Reservation. The boys were not thinking in those historical terms. They walked through the camp, admired the beautiful horses, and talked to the troopers in their blue uniforms. The troopers were friendly and ready to talk to two young boys who obviously were in awe of everything having to do with the cavalry.

"What is your name?" Scott asked the uniformed man with a sword, obviously an officer, who stood in front of the Company B row of tents.

"I'm Lieutenant O Brien, young man. I am a leader of the third platoon in Company B. And what is your name?

"I am Scott McCormick and he is Swallow No-Water," Scott replied and suddenly wondered if he should mention that Swallow was a Sioux Indian, but decided against it. No reason to bring up that subject.

"Do you really use that sword just like General Custer?" Scott queried the lieutenant.

"Well, yes and no," he replied to the young boy who was standing nose-to-nose with him and so close he was virtually standing on the Lieutenant's toes. "I do use it when giving commands and when the troop is at present-arms honoring the colors, but nowadays the sword is used more for tradition and in ceremonies than as a weapon. If I draw it from the scabbard, would you like to hold it?"

"Wow! Could I?" Scott responded, and reached for the sword even before it had cleared the scabbard.

"Hold it this way," the Lieutenant cautioned as he lifted it by the handle and carefully raised it with the blade out to the side and away from Scott and Swallow. Scott took it by the handle and raised it out to the side exactly the same way as the lieutenant. He carefully inspected it and ran his fingers along the blade to gauge its sharpness. Then he handed it to Swallow who did the same and handed it back to the lieutenant who returned it to his scabbard.

"Lieutenant O'Brien, who are your new friends?" asked an officer who had just then walked up.

"Sir, they are Scott McCormick and Swallow No-Water," he replied, obviously addressing a superior officer.

"Who are you," Scott asked the tall handsome man who wore a cavalry officer's hat and several medals that hung on his uniform blouse.

"I am Captain Rogers, the Company B commander. Pleased to meet you Scott and Swallow. Swallow No-Water: I'm guessing from your name that you are a Sioux Indian?"

"Yeah, I'm a mixed-blood Sioux."

"Swallow. Pleased to have you visit our camp and meet some of the troopers. We hold your Sioux tribe in high respect. Do you live on the Reservation?"

"Yeah," responded Swallow who was not anxious to visit with a cavalry officer. "But I am living here in Buffalo Gap while my dad is working on a ranch. We spend winters on the Pine Ridge Indian Reservation." As he responded he dropped his voice lower to a near whisper and hoped that would be the end of the interrogation.

"Well Scott and Swallow, pleased to have you tour our camp. This row of tents you are in is the bivouac for my Company B. Enjoy your selves and feel free to go over to the picket area and see some of our beautiful horses." Then he turned and walked away.

The two boys walked along the Company B row of pup tents about twenty in number with two men to each tent. They stopped in front of one where a trooper was unpacking the bedroll he had removed from his horse.

"I like your sleeping bag, it looks real comfortable" Scott declared.

"It's good for sleeping after riding all day," the trooper replied, looking up to see who was doing the interrogation.

"Is it waterproof?"

"No, we have a tent over our head to handle any rain. But if it starts to rain before we get the tents up, it can get pretty miserable."

"What about in the winter. Is it warm sleeping in a sleeping bag in the snow when it gets below zero?" The trooper's sleeping bag was the first Scott had ever seen and maybe someday he could have one for himself; all he ever used was a blanket and tarp.

"What's your name," Scott asked the trooper.

"Sergeant Kemp. And what are your names?"

"I am Scott McCormick, and he is Swallow No-Water."

"No-Water. Are you Sioux?"

"Yeah, I'm part Sioux," Swallow replied.

"Well, Swallow; meet another mixed-blood Indian. My father is white but my mother was Cherokee; so Swallow, we are both mixed-bloods, and I'm proud of it. I hope you are proud too." He reached his hand out to Swallow for a handshake. Swallow hesitated, not knowing the handshake procedure, but then extended his hand to the trooper.

"I guess I might be proud, but I've never thought about it. I am whatever I am and can't change that. I'd rather be white; they live better than we Indians do on the reservation. Anyway, since you are part Indian, why did you join the cavalry?"

"Because it is a job and even pretty good job. They feed us well in the cavalry and we don't work hard. I suppose if I still lived in Oklahoma where I come from, I would be digging ditch or something worse, but even riding a horse all day can get old after a while."

"But you kill people in the cavalry," retorted Swallow. "My granddad No-Water said the Seventh Cavalry killed his wife at Wounded Knee. She was my grandmother."

"I'm sorry about that, Swallow. It was a long time ago before I knew anything about the cavalry and I had nothing to do with it; we have never killed anyone since I've been in."

Scott wanted to change the subject that was getting a bit heavy. He would never have brought Swallow along if he knew the talk would become like this.

"Is that your rifle," asked Scott, changing the subject, and pointing to the trooper's rifle leaning against a tent pole."

"Yes. Do you want to hold it?"

"Awesome! Can I?"

"Okay." The trooper lifted the rifle, opened the bolt to insure it was empty with no bullet and held it out to Scott.

"Here, hold it carefully," He said handing it to Scott. "I have opened the bolt to insure it is not loaded. Point the barrel at the ground or up in the air and never at anyone. Boys, always treat a rifle with respect." Scott accepted the rifle and looked it over in considerable detail. It was the first one he had ever held and was surprised it was so heavy. Then he handed it to Swallow. Scott returned the rifle to the trooper, thanked him, and he and Swallow walked to the horse picket area that was down next to the gully with the cottonwood trees where he and his school classmates sometimes ate their noon lunch in the shade. They walked around the perimeter of the horses that numbered three hundred and were picketed in groups according to the horse color of their company.

As the sun began to set, the boys knew it was time to head for home. For Swallow it had been a disturbing time talking to his Grandfather's enemy; for Scott it had been one of his best days ever. Wow! He had been with the Seventh Cavalry and had talked with Captain Roger, a company commander, and he had even been saluted by the Colonel. He would have to tell his dad about that. It was amazing!

STANDING CLOSE TO THE
PRESIDENT—"OH MY GOSH!"

Travelling from Buffalo Gap to Rapid City was a big thing. Only fifty miles, but those miles were rutted dirt roads that were impassible if a bridge was out or after a heavy rain. And Rapid City itself was an experience for someone from a jerk-water town like Buffalo Gap. It had paved streets, signs on every corner with the name of a street like St. Joseph Avenue, Mount Rushmore Drive -- fancy names like that. There were boulevards with beautiful two-story mansions or at least they were mansions compared to the small fame houses in Buffalo Gap. And best of all, the iconic Alex Johnson soared over the town, a ten story hotel that was the social, political, and commercial center of Western South Dakota. Rapid City's impact was huge.

Franklin Delano Roosevelt had just been reelected for a second term as President of the United States, and he was coming to Rapid City. Even though Scott's dad was a Republican and not a fan of Roosevelt's, he decided it was a sufficient historic event that the family should make the trip to Rapid City to see him.

By this time, Scott's dad had traded in his 1933 Model A Ford for a 1936 Chevy. The family could now travel in comfort, even though it lacked some things of more expensive cars like a radio and air conditioning. Except for the Nolan's Buick, no car in town had air conditioning and theirs consisted of a swamp cooler mounted on the passenger side window.

The family left early to get a good spot. It was a beautiful morning for the drive. Floyd Thurston had graded the dirt road to Fairburn the day before, so the ruts from the last rain storm were minimal and the Chevy glided smoothly at 35 miles per hour, the top speed decreed by Scot's dad for his car on dirt roads. Arriving in Rapid City, Scott's dad drove down St. Joseph Avenue and parked. The family rushed to the Alex Johnson Hotel just in time to occupy the front spot behind the rope the Secret Service had erected to maintain a passage for the President from his car into the hotel. Scott stood behind the rope looking at all the people who had showed up; there were more people standing on the sidewalk alongside him than the total population of Buffalo Gap.

Scott heard a siren and down the street came the President in an open Cadillac convertible. Roosevelt and the South Dakota Governor sat in the back seat smiling and waving to the people. The convertible stopped in front of the hotel. A half-dozen Secret Service men got out of the trailing car and rushed to the convertible. Two agents lifted the President to his feet; it was apparent that Roosevelt could not stand unassisted or walk. Together the group exited the auto and agents carried Roosevelt by his arms into the hotel, while he smiled and waved to the crowd. The family had driven two hours from Buffalo Gap, stood in line for another two hours at the entrance to the Alex Johnson Hotel, and got to see Roosevelt for less than sixty seconds. Oh well, at least Scott got to see him and was in the front row where he was only five feet away and could almost touch him. Back home in Buffalo Gap, he could tell everyone that he had seen President Roosevelt close enough to touch. It was maybe the only time in his life he could see the President of the United States. It was epic.

MOUNTAIN LIONS FOR NEIGHBORS?

Scott was excited! Everybody loves bacon and pancakes, especially over a campfire. This was his first Boy Scout hike, first time cooking over a campfire, and first time in the bowels of wild Knapp's Canyon. The canyon was a deep gorge where prairie suddenly runs up against steep cliffs and the Black Hills begin.

Scott's home town, Buffalo Gap, sits alongside the little creek that flowed down from the mountains; but you probably never heard of Buffalo Gap -- it wasn't much even as South Dakota towns go -- only one hundred eighty seven people and seven of those were Scott's own family.

Yes, it was a small town, but it had a great Boy Scout troop, and Scott was a new tenderfoot with his sights already set on becoming an Eagle Scout -- just like his brother. It was the biggest thing in his life. Hiking across the prairie with the scout troop, they saw a coyote looping across a rise and down into a ravine. Then the troop reached the bottom of the cliffs and headed into the canyon. There were only deer trails to follow, and the climbing was tough. It was wild country. Scott had lain in bed many nights listening to the scream of mountain lions from the mountains, and their tracks with the claw marks were along the trail. Tonight, he would be camping with those big cats as his neighbor.

Scott carried rolled-up blanket for a bedroll on his shoulder and a sack slung over his back with a frying pan, food, and jug of water. On his belt he carried a knife and hatchet. In the 1930's, scouts had no mess kits, canteens, sleeping bags, or fancy things like that -- at least no one in Buffalo Gap had them.

The scoutmaster picked a campsite in a clearing that overlooked the nearly impassable bottom of the canyon. The older scouts made a pine bough lean-to in case of rain, but if it was a clear night they would be curled up in blankets under the stars.

First came supper. Scott gathered small firewood for cooking and bigger logs for a campfire after dark. With the help of another scout and two matches, he got a fire going. Scott was hungry, threw a slab of bacon into the frying pan and held it down over the flames. It started to sizzle, and then splatter. ... and it was nearly a disaster. He did not know you had to cook bacon slowly.

"Scott, raise the frying pan higher," warned the scoutmaster. "Bacon has to be cooked slowly; otherwise it will all burn up." He learned the first lesson in cooking over a campfire: know when to cook slowly and when over a hot flame.

Now for the pancakes. They were a standard bill of fare for his family during the 1930s -- either for breakfast or supper several times a week. The hungry kids needed lots of cheap fuel to keep their legs moving and may not have survived except for Aunt Jemima's pancake flour. For the same reason, it was ideal on a hikes and every Boy Scout learned to mix the batter and cook frying-pan size cakes.

They bought the pancake flour and most other groceries at John Degnan's store. Buffalo Gap hasn't had a grocery store for fifty years, but back in those days before the town dried up, it had three: Phillips, Towers, and Degnan's. Since his dad was the town banker, he had to patronize all three and pass his business around -- what little the family had available to pass. Mother baked bread, they got fruit and vegetables from the orchard and garden, and his mother spent most the summer canning and filling Mason jars for the long winter ahead.

The family got milk from the Bill Sewright ranch next door. Bill had eight milk cows and a bull, which he pastured a mile east of town. Scott would usually saddle up his horse, Buck, and herd the cows to and from pasture, and even help with the milking during the summer. Bill Sewright did not need the milk from the cows for drinking -- it was for the cream that came out of the separator. Cream was Mollie Sewright's money crop, and the left-over skim milk was a nearly worthless by-product. So Scott's family always had plenty of cheap milk, and what they didn't use, Bill

Sewright would feed to his hogs. With five kids, the family drank a lot of skim milk.

Scott needed a hot fire for the pancakes, so he threw on small limbs with pitch, placed the frying pan down close over the flames, and poured in enough batter for one pancake. It sizzled and when bubbles started to form on the topside, it was time to flip it over. That's when the scoutmaster came to his aid and demonstrated with the first pancake. He freed the pancake from the pan by swishing it back and forth; when it was free, he jerked the pan upward and the pancake went flying through the air above the pan. With the skill of a juggler, he caught the cake with the uncooked side against the hot pan. Now down over the fire again to cook the other side. Using a jackknife, he'd peek under the edge and see when it turns a golden brown.

Wow! Bacon and pancakes, and his first scout hike; it doesn't get any better than that, but he sure hoped that mountain lion would be quiet tonight.

The troop sat on logs around the campfire and told stories and sang scout songs. Scott grew sleepy. When the sun sank below the high cliffs and darkness crept in, he knew it was time to call it a day. The boys formed a circle with arms on the shoulders of each other, and they sang the song that had been sung around campfires for decades to the refrain of taps.

> *Day is gone.*
> *Gone the sun,*
> *From the plains,*
> *From the hills,*
> *From the sky.*
>
> *All is well.*
> *Safely rest,*
> *God is neigh.*

The coyotes were signing to the moon, but the mountain lion was quiet. Knowing God was neigh, Scott felt secure. Crawling under the blanket, he fell asleep before even remembering to count the stars.

12

ENCOUNTER WITH THE
GRIST MILL GHOST!

"Scott, do you want to explore the old Hennie Mill?" asked his older brother, Edwin.

"Great! Sure I do," Scott replied enthusiastically. Actually, he was hesitant and did not really want to do it, but Edwin seldom invited Scott to go anyplace with him, so he was quick to accept.

No kids in Buffalo Gap ever explored the abandoned building, and Scott would be scared; it was haunted by the ghost of old man Hennie. Once, late at night when the full moon was shining, two boys saw his ghost on the roof. When someone said it was only a hoot owl with big eyes that was sitting on the ledge, they responded that an owl could not wander all over the roof and then scramble through a broken window and climb into the top floor of the mill. And furthermore, some kids reported strange sounds of old-man Hennie moaning that came from the old mill late at night when his ghost was upset with the howling wind.

The grist mill had been closed for a dozen years since the death of the old man. After business went bad and the mill fell into hard times, Henne died suddenly; some said it was because he hung himself – the obituary in the Buffalo Gap Gazette said only that he had died but did not say how. After the funeral, his widow had all the doors of the mill padlocked; windows were boarded up, and she never allowed anyone to enter again. An eccentric, she still lived in the house in front of the mill and was a sentinel to keep everyone away – perhaps protecting them from his ghost.

"But I don't think we can even get inside the mill. It is locked shut by old lady Hennie," Scott added.

"We can get in," answered Edwin. "I know a secret way. Dennis and I explored inside the mill a couple years ago, but you've got to promise you won't tell anyone about it. The building is posted 'No Trespassing' and Dad and Mom would be upset if they learned. We could get in trouble."

Dennis and Edwin were several years older than Scott and seldom included him in what they did. Now Dennis was in the Navy, and apparently Edwin wanted to explore the mill again but was afraid to do it alone and needed the company of his young brother for the adventure.

The Henne Grist Mill was the biggest business in Buffalo Gap for many years; its three-story silhouette towered over the other buildings in town. All the farmers took their wheat to the mill to be ground-up and processed into flour. It was a terrible loss to the town when Henne died and his widow closed the mill; suddenly the farmers lost the local outlet for their products and their only alternative was to take the wheat to Nolan's grain elevator next to the railroad tracks to be shipped to Omaha. The widow Henne declared the mill would never operate again as long as she was alive.

"But, Edwin, how are we going to get into the mill to explore it?" Scott asked perplexed. "It's all padlocked and all the windows are boarded up. There is no way inside."

"I've been in it before. I know a secret way to enter, but if you come with me, you've got to promise to keep it secret."

"Okay," Scott responded. He figured the reason Edwin wanted him along was because it was an adventure no one wanted to undertake alone. Scott didn't know if it was really haunted by the ghost of Hennie, like all the kids in town said, but the insides of the mill might be dangerous. It would be dark, creepy with endless rooms, treacherous stairways, and hazardous storage bins everyplace -- and what if the ghost of old man Henne was still haunting the place?

Another reason the mill would never operate again was because the ditch that carried water from a dam on Beaver Creek became stilted with mud so little water flowed any more. It was water from the mill stream falling down onto a huge water wheel that powered the operations of the mill. A huge belt ran from the water wheel under the mill to the upper floors and engaged with other wheels and belts to operate the grain elevator that carried the product up to the top. Then grinders, shifters, blowers, mashers, and other machines converted the wheat into flour products.

"Okay, Scott, let's go. We need to take a flashlight because inside the mill it is too dark to see anything or where you are going. And we need a ball of kite string to mark our way as we move from room to room so we can follow the string back out again. Dennis and I forgot to take kite string. We got lost inside and thought we'd never find our way out again."

Edwin led the way to the mill. They sneaked around the side of widow Henne's house under her windows so she could not see them and crawled down the steep embankment alongside the mill to the water wheel that was underneath. The water wheel was huge, fifteen feet in diameter. It was the first time Scott had ever seen it. Located above the wheel was a spout where water from the mill stream fell down into the compartments that lined the wheel like steps on a ladder. As these buckets filled with water, the weight of the water caused the wheel to rotate, going round –and-round. As the buckets moved up on the other side and became upside-down, the water flowed out leaving them empty and ready to be filled again when they reached the top of the wheel in their rotation.

"You see, Scott, the water coming from the mill stream drops down into the buckets and the weight causes the wheel to rotate. That wide belt attached to the water wheel revolves along with it. The moving belt goes up through that hole into the floor above," Edwin explained. "So it is that belt that supplies all the power on the upper floors to make everything work. Isn't that neat?"

"Wow! I never saw a water wheel before. I didn't know they could do that. And all the water to operate the mill comes from the Kroth dam on Beaver Creek? That's awesome."

"Okay, now for the secret of how to get inside," whispered Edwin, although no one else was there to hear. "See that hole above the water wheel where the belt goes into the floors above; well, that hole's the secret. We'll crawl up through that hole and push the belt aside. We can use the wheel like a step ladder and stand on top and lift ourselves up through the hole. I'll go first and you follow me."

Scott climbed up the water wheel after Edwin and pulled himself up through the hole. It was a tight squeeze next to the belt. His brother reached a hand down to help him up through the hole. After he scrambled to his feet in the darkness, Scott stood next to Edwin who was waiting for him with a flashlight and ball of kite string. He handed the ball of kite string to Scott.

"Tie the end of the kite string to this brace by the opening and as we walk along, Scott, you feed out the string so we will be able to follow it back here again and won't get lost in the darkness like Dennis and I did. We almost never made it out and considered breaking a boarded-up window to get out. That would really have gotten us into trouble."

Edwin scanned the darkness with the beam of his flashlight. The place was filled with spider webs that hung from the ceiling and corners, and the floor was littered with rat droppings. "See that set of wheels over there. The belt from the water wheel rotates that other belt going up through that hole to the upper floors. It pulls the elevator conveyor that lifts all the wheat from the farmer's trucks up to the top floor where the wheat is stored in bins and ready to be processed. Now follow me and remember to feed out the kite string as we go along." Edwin moved up a stairway flashing his flashlight ahead in the darkness. With only the one flashlight, Scott was left in darkness to stumble along behind his brother. His face and hair were quickly covered with spider webs that filled the stairwell; Scott was already wishing he had not come.

At the top of the stairwell, they exited into an enclosure that had trap doors leading into a half dozen bins. Peering into one bin, the flashlight beam caught a huge rat; it quickly scurried away into a dark corner. Edwin decided to not investigate inside any more bins; one rat was enough. Another stairway led above and they took off again.

"Edwin, wait for me. You've got the only flashlight and I can't see anything in the dark. I can't keep up with you because I've got to take time to unwind and feed out this kite string. It keeps getting all tangled up. We sure don't want to get lost in this dungeon."

"Okay, but keep up. We've got a lot of exploring to do," he declared as he climbed the narrow stairway. Half way up the stairs, he stopped. There in the beam of his flashlight sitting on a step sat a raccoon. Edwin yelled and it scurried up the stairs ahead of them and disappeared. The top floor had another dozen bins with trap doors where the wheat would be stored before starting the processing. "Okay, this is the top floor."

As they stood in total darkness, suddenly there was a sound from above, perhaps on the roof, and a hoot –like that from an owl -- and a soft whisper or murmur, perhaps from wind blowing through a broken window, but was it only the wind? Scott stood listening, spellbound with fear. Was this Henne's ghost?

"Edwin, do you hear what I hear?"

"I don't hear anything, just stuff rattling on the roof and wind blowing through a hole someplace. It's nothing."

"I'm not so sure. It doesn't sound like anything I've heard before. Are you sure what it is?"

"Yeah, it's just the wind and a bunch of varmints like the rats running around up here. Maybe it's a raccoon; there are probably a lot of them in this abandoned building that make it their home. I know all the stories about Henne's ghost. Scott, there is no such things as a ghost."

"I'm not so sure about that. I've read stories about them and I believe in them. Old man Henne hung himself, so maybe he is wandering around up here trying to hide from God who is mad at him. Maybe he even hung himself in this room. That beam up there in the ceiling could be where he tied the rope with the hangman noose. Look at that stuff hanging from the beam. I wonder is it's the same rope?"

"Well, I don't believe in all that stuff. Anyway, Scott, now we've got to cross over to the other side where all the processing was done in the mill to make flour."

"How do we get over there?" Scott asked.

"We crawl on our hands and knees through this narrow tunnel. It is a passageway over the top of the truck ramp below. Over on the other side is where the real work of the mill gets done."

Scott followed Edwin on his hands and knees and crawled through the tunnel. He felt the slime and rat droppings on the bottom of the tunnel. He held his nose, but was getting covered with the stuff. At the other end of the tunnel, Edwin was waiting with his flashlight scanning a large room. The flashlight was growing dimmer as the batteries gradually wore out, leaving them in near total darkness. Silhouettes of a dozen large machines interconnected with a maze of tubes, pipes, braces, and power belts. It looked like a dungeon he'd seen in a movie.

"See that machine over there," Edwin said pointing with his flashlight beam. "That is a grinder. The wheat that is transported through that pipe from the other side of the mill goes into that machine and the kernels get ground up into smaller pieces. Dennis explained it all to me; he came through the mill with Dad before it got shut down. Then it gets blown into that pipe over there and goes to that other grinder where it is made even finer." Edwin obviously knew what he was talking about. During their previous exploration, Dennis had explained everything to him.

"Then the ground-up wheat is passed through the pipes over there into the two blowing machines located back there that separate the wheat germ from the brand. Each of them sends their product into collector bins. See those machines over there?" he asked as he pointed the flashlight beam. "They are the sifters. That is where a lot of stuff like weed seeds and chaff is filtered out. Then the final job is done by the mashers back there along the back wall that pound and pulverizes the kernels into flour."

The brothers felt their way to each machine and using his flashlight Edwin explained how each worked. It became obvious from sounds around their feet that they were not alone, and they heard the rustle of rats and other noises as they scurried from one end to the other of the darkened room. The left-over wheat scattered over the floor had supplied a lifetime of food for rats and other varmints.

"Now we'll go down another flight of stairs to the diesel room," Edwin announced as he headed down another narrow stairwell and Scott stumbled along behind in the darkness. At the bottom it exited into a small room almost completely filled with a huge diesel generator. "This is the diesel engine. It operates on diesel fuel and provides the power for all the processing machines. There isn't enough water from Beaver Creek for the water wheel to do anything except transport the wheat from the farmer's trucks to the top floor where gravity can take over. But the processing machines require a lot of power and that's the purpose of this diesel engine." Edwin stopped his explanation. "Scott, you're not holding the ball of kite string. Where is it?"

"I ran out of string."

"You ran out? My God! How are we going to find our way out?"

"Well, the ball of kite string ran out in the middle of that tunnel and I didn't have any more. I was too busy crawling through that tunnel to say anything or do anything about it. So, all we have to do is find our way back to that tunnel and we'll find the end of the kite string."

"Damn it, Scott! I sure hope we can find our way back to that tunnel in the dark. The batteries in this flashlight are dead. It will be impossible to find our route through that big room with all the processing machines, pipes, belts, and everything." Edwin led the way up the stairs into the processing floor. By following the flow of machines in the reverse order, they were able to reach the tunnel. As they crawled through on their hands and knees, halfway across they found the end of the kite string and followed it through the tunnel.

"This is the top floor where we saw that raccoon and you thought you heard old man Henne's ghost up on the roof. That noise might have been an owl or raccoons," Edwin said. "I'm going to look through this trap door and see if we can get another look at the raccoon." He raised the trap door with his left arm and held the flashlight inside and searched with its beam. Suddenly, he yelled and dropped the flashlight as the door slammed shut. "Yeaow! Damn it! I've dropped the flashlight inside. I felt something. It might have been Henne's ghost, but I doubt it. I was afraid something inside there was about grab me or bit me. I'm not climbing into that bin in total darkness to look for the flashlight when it's got something in there. Scott, we'll just have to follow the kite string in the dark back to the opening at the water wheel three floors below."

Edwin led the way as he followed the kite string and Scott walked behind in the total darkness. "Stay close with your hands on my shoulders, Scott, and don't stumble on the stairs. We're on the second floor now and only one more flight of stairs to get through."

At last they reached the belt hole in the bottom floor. Letting themselves down to the top of the water wheel they clambered down to solid ground. It was already getting dark so they scurried home. As they entered the lighted kitchen, they saw they were covered with spider webs and dirt from head to toe.

"My God!" exclaimed their mother. "You boys are covered with dirt and filth. What have you been doing?"

Scott stood silent. He was sworn to secrecy. He wouldn't know what to say. It was Edwin's job to make excuses.

"Mother, we were doing some exploring and got dirty, just like Dennis and I did two years ago."

"And young man, where was that?" she asked in a severe tone of voice

"Mother, I can't say. I took an oath to Dennis that we would keep it secret when we were exploring two years ago, so I'm sworn to secrecy and can't tell you. I'll take the blame, along with Dennis, so punish me, and not Scott."

"Well, your punishment will be outside." With that statement, she led us outside to the edge of the vegetable garden and she hooked up the hose to the outside faucet. As we stood naked, she sprayed us from head to foot. It was mighty cold water, particular since we were naked and shivering. Scott wasn't sure if it was for punishment or to get clean, but either way, it served its purpose. One encounter with the ghost of old-man Henne was enough. Scott never had the urge to go back inside that grist mill again.

"SCOTT, HOLD A TIGHT REIN, AND STAY CLOSE!"

"Cowboys, rise and shine!" announced Rex's father, Joe Norman, in a loud voice as he stood at the door of his ranch bunkhouse. "It's roundup time today when all cowboys have to be in the saddle. After you get dressed, breakfast will be waiting for you in the kitchen. Now out of bed and into those boots!"

Scott awoke from a sound sleep. He scarcely remembered where he was; then saw the cots where Rex and Swallow were slowly starting to move. Joe Norman had invited Scott and Swallow to join Rex at the spring roundup as a special time for the three boys whose fathers often had business together.

Only last year, Scott had ridden a horse for the first time with Pop Bill Sewright when herding the milk cows to the pasture east of Buffalo Gap. Now he had been invited to join Rex and Swallow at the Norman Ranch for the annual spring roundup. The boys were excited to be sleeping together in the bunkhouse, talking far into the night in anticipation of the big day ahead. The day had arrived.

Scott was the first out of his cot. "Hurry up guys, we don't want to miss this big day," he declared. His friends showed no sign of movement. "I'm hungry. Need to get some food in me."

"It is so early, I'm not sure I can talk my stomach into eating," allowed Swallow. "It's still dark. My God! What time is it?"

"It's probably about five-thirty," stated Rex. "My dad usually gets up by this time, especially on a day when there is riding to do. We'd better hurry over to the kitchen for some breakfast or he'll get upset."

Rex's mother, Alice Norman, was in the kitchen pouring her husband a cup of coffee as the boys walked in. She gave them a big smile. "Here come three cowboys who look hungry. I'll bet you can eat a couple pancakes, some bacon, and a couple eggs," she declared. With three boys at her kitchen table, this was an exceptional day for her. Their parents were family friends, so she knew the boys well. "Scott, I'll start with you. Are you ready to try one of my piping hot pancakes?"

"Yes, ma'am, I sure am," Scott replied, even though he wasn't sure he was ready to eat while it was still dark outside but knew he'd better try, because it might be a long time until the next meal.

Joe Norman was sitting at the table having finished his breakfast and was sipping from his coffee cup. "Well, boys, this is it, the big day, the spring roundup. I hope you are ready to do some riding today; we've got over a thousand head of calves to brand." Taking a last sip from his coffee cup, he pushed his chair back from the table and stood up. "Boys, I'm heading out. You're on your own to get saddled-up and on the way. The hired hand Mike will help you with the horses. He's already got a horse picked out for Scott and Swallow, and they are in the corral with Rex's horse. Boys, I'll see you at the Sioux Corrals. Rex, you know the way to those corrals across the river toward the Indian Reservation where the roundup is always held." With that brief comment, he left.

After finishing their breakfast, the boys headed to the horse corral. On the way Scott announced, "I'm a bit scared. I'm not a good rider like you guys are. I can ride, but not real good. I hope I can keep up with you guys."

"Scott, you will do just fine." Rex responded in a patronizing voice. "You are probably better than you think you are, and if you need any help, Swallow and I will be right there with you."

Last night in the bunkhouse, they talked late into the night firming up their new friendship. Scott and Rex had known each other since early childhood, and Swallow since last year, but this was the first time they had ever slept together in the same room. Rex Norman was raised on his father's ranch alongside the Cheyenne River. Swallow No-Water was an

Indian boy who lived on his father's ranchero on the Pine Ridge Indian Reservation. Scott McCormick was the banker's son raised in Buffalo Gap. They had been raised in three different cultures: a ranch in the Cheyenne River Country, the town of Buffalo Gap, and on the Pine Ridge Indian Reservation.

The boys walked to the horse corrals where Rex and Swallow caught their horses and began to put on bridles and saddles. The hired-hand, Mike, caught a horse for Scott.

"His name is Cheyenne." Mike announced. "He's a good horse, fairly gentle, and a good one for you," he said to give Scott confidence since he was an inexperienced rider. "You will like Paint. I ride him a lot. He will not buck, and is a good totter to keep up on the trail." Scott took hold of the reins and looked at the horse's eyes that glared back at him with a frightened look, so Scott rubbed the horse's nose and patted his shoulder. Gradually the horse settled down and stopped shivering. Mike put on the saddle blanket and lifted the saddle onto the back of the horse. Scott reached under the belly for the cinch, fed it through the buckle and tightened it up, just like he had learned last summer from Pop Bill Sewright.

The only previous horseback riding Scott had done was with Pop Bill when he herded milk cows to the pasture east of Buffalo Gap, and when riding ponies bareback with Swallow. Herding cows was not difficult riding, but Scott had to drive them through the back alleys of Buffalo Gap, across the railroad tracks, through Beaver Creek and up the hill east of town to their pasture. At night, he would ride to the pasture, round them up, and bring them back. The cows would usually be waiting near the gate, but sometime they were scattered elsewhere in the pasture and he had to search through all the ravines to find them. Sometimes this took over an hour, so Scott got extra riding on those days. He had some riding experience, but nothing like Rex and Swallow who had been riding since they were old enough to walk.

Mike opened the corral gate and the boys were off. "Rex, you know the way to the Sioux Corrals," declared Mike, but he felt it well to review since they were not easy to find. "It is down the ravine to the sand bar crossing where Lame Johnny Creek flows into the Cheyenne River. Cross through the river, it will be only knee deep to the horses, take the trail east toward the Indian Reservation to the Sioux Corrals. It is trail all the way and won't be hard to find. Rex, you know the way."

Rex led the way out the ranch yard at a trot. The first half mile was a trail gradually sloping downward through a series of ravines and the breaks of the river. The Cheyenne River that meandered through a wide valley in this part of the country could be a raging torrent in the early spring with the snow melt, but by this time of the summer was seldom over knee deep. As the boys headed their horses down the embankment to the river, Rex ran his horse straight into the shallow water without stopping and barely slowed as he raced through the water and up the steep bank on the other side. Swallow was right behind him. Scott hung on to the saddle horn as his horse entered the river, and he grabbed the leather straps as the horse lurched up the steep embankment on the other side where the other guys sat on a bluff waiting for him.

"Rex, wait up," Scott yelled. "I'm not a good rider like you guys." Rex pulled his horse to a stop, stood tall in his stirrups, turned and waved to Scott.

"Hey, Dude. We know that. But you aren't half bad for a city guy, and a banker's son on top of that."

He called Scott 'Dude' – a belittling name for a new cowboy. Scott had a feeling it might be his new nickname and did not like it, but knew he had no choice since he really was a dude

Scott rode up the bluff alongside the others and the three started walking side-by-side on their horses eastward along the trail in the direction of the Indian Reservation, Rex in the middle leading the way. They chatted as they walked along. Scott and Rex were the sons of the two most prominent men in this part of the country. Rex's dad, Joe Norman, was the biggest rancher on the open range with thousands of cattle that roamed the fenceless territory from the Badlands in the north, east across the Pine Ridge Indian Reservation and south to the Nebraska border -- no fences anywhere until reaching the Nebraska State Line. Everyone respected Joe and the ranchers always appointed him as the Roundup Boss. It was a job with tough responsibilities, because he had to make the final decisions whenever there was conflict or a debate over whose calf belonged to which rancher. Joe's decisions were never challenged by the other ranchers. It was also his job to organize the roundups and that took some experience. When the ranchers got together on the appointed day, they had already rounded up a couple thousand head of cattle from all over the prairie, and drove them to the Sioux Corral. It took several days of hard riding. The cowboys rode cutting horses to separate the cows and calves of each rancher into separate corrals so each calf could be identified and branded with the owner's brand. The roundup would be a long day with lots of cowboy work to do.

Joe Norman also had to keep organization in the branding arena that was filled with numerous cowboys. Three crews with six cowboys on horses did the roping, while others on foot maintained branding fires that kept the branding irons hot. Another half-dozen cowboys worked with the ropers throwing the calves to the ground and tying down their legs so they laid still and could be branded. Other cowboys did the actual branding by pressing the hot branding iron against the hip of the calf. The calves did not like it, kicking, struggling and bawling violently. It was work that required a strong cowboy who could manhandle the calves. Another dozen cowboys worked in the corrals behind the chutes feeding the calves into the arena. There were often a hundred cowboys involved in the roundup.

Swallow's father was George No-Water, who had a small spread with a few cattle on the Pine Ridge Indian Reservation. Swallow's grandfather had been a chieftain during the decades before the Sioux were forced onto the reservation. George ran a cattle camp up on the Cuny Table plateau that rose several hundred feet above the Badlands near the center of the Reservation. He had grown into manhood as someone respected by all the other Indians and also by the white ranchers living adjacent to the Reservation who knew him. Most of them were mixed-blood Sioux the same as George. They relied on him to protect their Indian interests even though they had less clout than the white ranchers.

Scott McCormick's father, Frank, ran the bank in Buffalo Gap and he was the glue that kept all the ranchers of the area financially solvent during these rough years of the 1930's Great Depression. They all had loans and mortgages from the bank to finance their ranches and cattle herds. During the year if the price of beef was down, it would be Scott's father in the bank who would keep the ranchers out of foreclosure. Scott and Rex's families were acquaintances, not just because of doing business together, but they were also friends who played gin rummy at each other's houses on Saturday nights and sat together in the church pews on Easter and Christmas.

It was still semi-dark on a cold morning, and the horses pulled at their bridles anxious to move faster to a trot. "Rex, everyone calls your dad the Roundup Boss. What does that mean?" Scott inquired.

"He's the guy who runs the roundup – the boss man. When there is an argument over who owns some calf, he makes the decision which rancher it belongs to."

"I suppose you guys have been to roundups before, but this is my first one," Scott said as he began to feel more comfortable in the saddle. With his horse at a trot and his feet solid in the stirrup, Scott began to move with a natural cadence rocking fore and aft with his horse, Paint. The hired hand was right, it was a good horse, a little lively but gentle enough that Scott was no longer worried about staying in the saddle even if the horse were to break into a gallop.

"You've never been to a roundup before? I've been to one every year since I was five," said Rex proudly as he leaned back in his saddle. "They are fun to watch, but this will be the first year that Swallow and I have been able to ride horses inside the corrals. You have never seen so many cowboys and ranchers in one place before. Everyone is there. All our Indian friends from the reservation are there along with ranchers from all over the Cheyenne River Country, even from up in Fairburn. A lot of them come just to watch the action or hang around the chuck wagon to eat the food."

Rex's horse suddenly shied sideways, perhaps spooked by a snake, but Rex quickly brought him under control.

"It's like some sort of celebration," Rex continued without hesitation. "It's like a carnival only more fun; but my dad doesn't have much fun, it is real work for him and he is always busy making decisions or getting everyone to hurry up and move faster so we can get all the calves branded before the end of the day when it gets too dark."

"Yeah, but why do they do it, what's the purpose of a roundup – what's it for?"

"Dude, it is necessary because during the winter cattle go everywhere on the open range and get all mixed up. They range from the Badlands many miles all the way down to Nebraska. There are no fences anywhere. The cattle are everywhere and the herds are all mixed up. You can't keep them separated. So after the calves are born in the spring, it's a question of who owns which calves." Rex paused to catch his breath. "See, that's the problem. In the spring after the calves are born the ranchers round up all the cattle in one central place like the Sioux Corrals next to the Cheyenne River and sort everything out. Every calf will always stay with its mother cow. So the cowboys rope the calf and put the same brand on it that the mother has on her rump, and so that way every rancher knows who owns what."

"Hey, that makes sense. Does it always work? What if some calf is running around without a mother cow?"

"That happens sometimes. It seems the cowboys figure things out -- I don't know how, but they usually do. Then if they can't, my dad looks things over, makes a decision, and assigns the calf to some rancher. See, all of this happens in one large corral that is full of cowboys roping, a half dozen branding fires, hundreds of calves bawling when the branding irons are burned into their rumps. Cowboys are swearing and yelling -- boy it is fun to watch."

But it still did not explain what these young boys would be doing, and Scott worried about that. They might be considered cowboys now, riding horses at the roundup, but doing what? "Okay, Rex, what do we do; just sit on our horses and watch, or do we do something?"

"My dad will tell us about that. There are usually too many cattle for the corrals, so some of the cowboys are needed to ride outside the herd and keep the cattle from running back into the open range. It sounds easy, but it isn't, because those cattle are always trying to escape. That is what we will probably start doing until there is room for all the cattle to fit inside the holding corrals."

The boys rode down a sharp ravine and up the other side where they reached the top of a bluff that was high ground. Ahead in the distance they could see a large herd, more cattle than Scott had ever seen before.

"There they are! -- the Sioux Corrals and the roundup." cried Rex. He was so excited he took off on a dead gallop and Swallow followed. Scott gave Paint his head and did the same. As Paint opened-up running at a full gallop, Scott was beginning to feel more comfortable in the saddle. Maybe he was becoming a real cowboy. As the boys grew closer, the Sioux Corrals became visible and an opening appeared through the herd. Joe Norman saw them coming and rode out to meet the boys. "Howdy, Boys. Glad you made it and you are just in time. We need you and I've got a job for the three of you. We've got so many cattle we can't keep them all inside the fences, so there is a herd on the south side that we've got to keep together or they will scatter back out to the prairie. I've got a couple cowboys on them now, but they need help. It's over there to the south. Ed Rangle is in charge. Rex, go find Ed and offer him your help. Okay, Boys?"

"Sure, Dad," responded Rex in a self-important voice. He led the way as they skirted around the outside of the herd. Ed Rangle asked them to ride the perimeter of the herd and head off any cows that tried to make a break for the outside. Scott watched Rex and Swallow take-up a patrol around the herd, so he did the same thing. The cattle were a loud and unruly bunch. None of them wanted to stay with the herd and every time some cow saw an opening, she'd dash at full speed out into open space. Rex and Swallow were good at urging their horses at top speed to get ahead of the cow, cut it off, and then yell as they chased her back into the herd. They held ropes in the free hand to swing at the rump of the cow as a gentle reminder of who was boss.

Scott began to master the whole experience. He could ride Paint good, anticipate when a cow was about to seek freedom, head it off, yell at them, and use his rope on their rump to remind them who was boss. It became fun.

After an hour all the cattle had been moved inside the fences, so the boy's job was completed. Joe Norman rode out and met them.

"Good job, boys. Thanks. Now come with me to the corral. Rex and Swallow, you tie your horses over there and sit on the top rail where you can watch the action. Scott, you come with me."

Rex did not like what he heard. Swallow and he would be sitting on the fence while Scott could ride his horse inside the branding corral with his father?

"Dad," said Rex. "His name is not Scott any more. We've got a new nickname for him. It's Dude."

"Dude? How do you know he'll like a name like that?" asked Joe. "Dude is fine with me," Scott replied. "I guess I'm a dude, so that name may be okay."

"It may be okay with you, but it's not with me. I don't like the name and before this day is out, you'll be a real cowboy. Scott, come with me," said Joe. "We'll ride inside the branding corral and get up close to the action. Just sit your horse, hold a tight rein, and stay close to me. We'll see how the roundup action is going." As they approached the gate, a cowboy on foot opened it so they could ride inside. Joe rode to a position alongside the fence where they stopped and sat on their horses. He kept Scott on the inside next to the fence away from the action, and began to explain what was going on. "Inside this corral we have a couple dozen men all doing their own job and working in three different roping crews. Each crew has two men who are roping calves and a half dozen other cowboys tying the calves down, dragging them, and using the branding irons. Each crew has a couple fires and men who are keeping them stoked-up and the branding irons hot. So there is a lot of action." The noise from the cattle was so loud Scott could hardly hear what Joe was saying.

"Over on the other side are a couple dozen cowboys outside the corral who are feeding the calves into the chutes. They have to separate the calves from their mothers, so it requires a good cutting horse. The calves don't want to cooperate, so it takes a good cowboy and a horse trained for the job."

"Once the calf is pushed out the chute, a roper throws a noose around its neck with his lariat, and another guy lifts the calf up and throws it to the ground and ties its legs. That takes a mighty strong guy who is manhandling a struggling calf. Then when the calf is lying on the ground and its legs tied, another guy brings the hot branding iron from the fire and burns the brand onto the rump of the calf – the same brand its mother has. That hot iron really gets their attention and all the bawling noise you hear is the result."

"Wow," Scott responded in amazement. "The calves really bellow when they feel the iron and the smoke flares up on their rump."

"It doesn't hurt them all that much," Joe said. "They have thick skins, but they are frightened. As soon as their legs are free and they jump up, they are all through. They are chased out those gates on the other side where they rejoin their mothers."

What a spectacle and Scott with a ring-side seat, sitting on his horse alongside Joe Norman, the roundup boss, inside the branding corral. It couldn't get any better; it was awesome. He counted at least thirty or forty cowboys inside the branding corral, each one busy with their own job. Scott was glad to be with Joe, because he was the round-up boss and in charge of all the action. Anyone inside that arena who did not know what he was doing could easily get hurt.

After a while, Joe said, "Okay, Scott, let's go outside and you can join Rex and Swallow on the top rail." The gate was opened for them and they rode out of the corral. Scott tied his horse to the fence and climbed up to joined Rex and Swallow on the top rail and watch the action.

Scott started counting the calves as they were branded. As near as he could figure, there were about four calves branded every minute and chased out of the corral by the three crews, so that would be a couple hundred calves per hour. Joe Norman said they wanted to brand about two thousand calves today, so it would take a very long day to get that done.

Around noon, Rex announced that he was hungry. "Let's find where the chuck wagon is set up and get something to eat." The boys rode their horses to a grove of cottonwood trees south of the corrals alongside the Cheyenne River where a group of women had tables set and stacked with food. It had been a long time since breakfast, and Scott was hungry. Rex's mother was in charge in charge of the chuck wagon lunch.

Then he saw someone he knew and was surprised to see Swallow's sister, Meadowlark. He had not seen her since their encounter last summer at the Sewright encampment. He was bashful around pretty girls, but wanted to go over and say hello.

"Hello, Meadowlark," he voiced as he walked up.

"Scott! What are you doing here?" she asked, delighted to see him.

"I'm helping with the roundup," he responded in a matter-of-fact voice, as if it was routine. She sure was a pretty girl; he had forgotten how cute she was. "I've been riding with Rex and Swallow, and we've been helping out. I was in the branding corral with Joe Norman, the roundup boss."

"Where did you get a horse? You could have borrowed my pony if you had asked me," she said teasing to egg him on.

"I'm riding one of Norman's horses, Cheyenne, and he's about twice as tall as your pony and I ride him with a saddle, not bareback." As soon as he said it, he realized that may be too much of a tease. "But maybe sometime I'll ask you if I can ride your pony again. I'd like to. You were so mad when you saw me riding it last time and bawling me out that you never did tell me your pony's name."

"I wasn't bawling you out. I was just upset because I didn't know you, and suddenly I saw some stranger riding my pony without my permission. I didn't know you back then, remember? My pony's name is Paint, and I'd like you to ride her again. You don't even have to ask me, I'm already giving you permission."

"Paint, that's a good name and fits exactly with a pinto pony. Okay, sometime I'll ask you for another ride." He didn't know where he got the courage to stand toe-to-toe and talk with a pretty girl without his usual stammering or being at a loss for words. "Well, I'd better go with Rex and Swallow and get some food in me. We've got a lot of work to do this afternoon. Goodbye, Meadowlark, I hope to see you at your camp again next summer."

"Goodbye, Cowboy. For sure, I'll be there and see you again."

Late in the afternoon the roundup was coming to an end as the corral emptied of calves and the branding fires were all going out. George No-Water, who had been one of the ropers, rode out the gate to where Joe Norman and the boys sat on their horses.

"Well, Joe, we managed to get it done," he announced with pride. "My crew gave me the count. Two thousand, one hundred, and thirty five calves branded today. Not a bad day's work."

"It sure wasn't," responded Joe.

"I'll get my Indian crew together and we'll start our herd in the direction of the Reservation. I'll drop over to your place in the morning and pick up Swallow, if it's alright for him to spend another night with Rex and Scott in your bunkhouse."

"Sure thing, George," said Joe. "I'll ride back to the ranch with the boys. We'll get a bite to eat and then I'll bet they'll be ready for some time in the bunk house. It's been a long day for them. See you in the morning when you come to pick up Swallow, and come in time for a cup of coffee and piece of Alice's apple pie. I told Mike to let my own herd scatter from here. It's as good a place as any. See you in the morning."

Then Joe turned to the boys. "Rex, you take the lead and let's ride up the Sioux trail to home. Scott and I will bring up the rear. It's getting dark, so we'd better not linger along the trail but just walk the horses, they're tired too." Rex and Swallow took off and Joe Norman and Scott followed along well behind.

"Well, Scott how did you like your first roundup?"

"Mister Norman, it was great -- one of my best days ever -- probably the most exciting day in my life. When you took me inside the branding corral, I thought I would die of fright because everything seemed so dangerous, but with you at my side and sitting on a good horse, I felt comfortable and safe. Thank you."

"Good, Scott. You did a good job. If you were frightened, it did not show at all. But with that corral full of cowboys roping and dragging, fires burning, calves being branded and kicking and struggling, it can be a mighty dangerous place, so you were wise to feel danger. But I would not let you be in any real danger. You noticed that I kept your horse pinned against the rails of the fence and I was always on the outside between you and the heavy action. Anyway, Scott; a good job. You earned you spurs today and are now a cowboy. No one should ever call you Dude again." He lightly spurred his horse in the flank to pick up the pace.

"Now it's starting to get dark so keep a tight rein on Cheyenne so he doesn't stumble with his footing. The moon is starting to rise and it will be dark before we get back to the ranch, but your eyes will adjust, and Paint knows the way."

Scott and Joe Norman started at a trot and fell silent. Scott was reliving the day as he headed for home. He felt good. Joe Norman had called him a real cowboy.

At the barn they removed the saddles, watered the horses, placed a half bucket of oats in each horse's stall trough, and headed into the ranch house. They were too tired to eat much and soon headed to the bunkhouse.

"Rex and Swallow, thanks for including me today for the roundup. That was the best day of my life. It was awesome." Scott closed his eyes and was fast asleep.

14

HE REPLACED HIS CACHE IN THE SECRET HIDING PLACE

Scott had climbed every ravine, canyon, and mountain west of Buffalo Gap, even into the bottom of the three canyons: Calico, Whetstone, and Knapp's; he'd hiked them with his older brothers. One spring during a heavy downpour that became a cloud bust, he ran with them through the flooded ravines of the prairie to Knapp's Canyon so they could see water gushing over the waterfall at the entrance to the canyon. Normally the waterfall was dry and this was their first chance to see a juggernaut cascading over the thirty foot cliff that guarded entry to the canyon. It was a frightening sight; the roar was deafening. They watched the deluge for an instant then dashed homeward back across the prairie before flash flooding would render the ravines impassable. It was his most exciting day ever with his big brothers – awesome.

After his brothers joined the navy and were gone, his only chance to go hiking again was to include his sister, Betty, as his parents would not let him go alone. She was a year younger but a good hiker and liked to hike with him.

On Saturday mornings they'd take off together with a sandwich and jug of water and head for the mountains. The first part was an easy hike crossing the mile of sage brush prairie west of town through the prairie dog town and barbed wire fence at the mountain's edge. That's where the climb would begin up the steep mountain where un-climbable cliffs awaited them at the top. Scott knew the way to evade the cliffs was by circling around their north flank on a Whetstone Canyon ridgeline. After they reached the top they sat on the edge of the cliff face, dangled their feet, and rested while admiring the view.

Buffalo Gap was a thousand feet below and two mile to the east. In the distance beyond the town was the Cheyenne River Country where his friend, Rex Conners, lived on a ranch. Further to the east through the haze they could see the outlines of the spires of Badland buttes. Cuny Table, where his friend Swallow No-Water lived, would be located in the Badlands on the Indian Reservation.

After resting, they continued the hike to the edge of Whetstone Canyon where an outcropping of whetstone rocks made for difficult hiking. It was an ancient Indian quarry where Sioux Indians fashioned the sharp stones of arrowheads, spears, and tomahawks they used as weapons. Walking through the quarry along the south shoulder of Whetstone Canyon, they came to a grassy plateau that separated the canyon from the upper part of Knapp's canyon to the south.

Scott knew from experience to avoid climbing up Knapp's canyon from the front-end entrance because of the waterfall cliff that was difficult to get around, but it was an easy climb down into mid-canyon using a route he'd discovered with his brother, Edwin. At the bottom was a spring with clear running water. They took a drink, re-filled their water jug, and ate their peanut butter-jelly sandwich. Scott and Betty liked to explore the bottom of Knapp's Canyon because it was such a beautiful place with a combination of spruce trees interspersed with quaking aspen that "sang" in a gentle breeze. Sometimes they even saw a herd of elk.

Betty was a good hiker. She could keep up with him and was always interested to explore the same things as Scott. Even though they had taken this hike before, there were always new things to discover.

From the bottom of Knapp's canyon, Scott knew the trail up the south side to their ultimate destination: Powell's Cabin. It was perched on the rim. No one knew who built the cabin or where it got its name. The cabin was tumbledown with a caved in roof and no windows or doors and had been abandoned for decades, perhaps since some early pioneer had become the victim of Sioux Indian warriors. Even though Scott had been to Powell's cabin many times before, he always spent time in a search for artifacts, but never found any. It had been looted for decades with no artifacts remaining. However, in the field alongside the cabin was an outcropping of petrified wood, and Scott and Betty spent an hour looking for a good specimen. Spring rains that washed away topsoil, sometimes revealed new petrified wood varieties. She found a beautiful one with crystalized contours. It was a keeper, and Scott knew he would have to carry it home; it was too heavy for Betty.

It was already afternoon and time to start back. Instead of taking the same route on the return, they followed around the tail end of Knapp's canyon to a large plateau that extended a half-mile all the way to the backside edge of Calico Canyon. They would circle around and find the trail that headed eastward across the plateau that would return them to the promontory on top of the cliffs where they had rested in the morning. When they got there, they were tired so they sat down and took in the view. The five mile hike had taken five hours; the sun they faced in the morning was now behind them and soon would be setting. Buffalo Gap far below was now in the shadow of the mountains.

The trail around the cliff and down the mountain side was easy, and half-way down Scott stopped at a huge boulder with a small recessed hollow in its side. This was the secret hiding place of his cache. Two years ago he hid a metal container that contained special artifacts he was saving as a secret time capsule to be opened in some future year. After swearing Betty to secrecy, he reached into the hiding place to retrieve his cache. Opening it, he found everything was still intact: a bone handle jackknife, 1895 silver dollar, Teddy Roosevelt campaign button his granddad gave him, blue ribbon he won in a race at school, several old nickels and pennies, and a faded family photo. He closed the container and replaced it out-of-sight in his secret hiding place in the hollow.

"Betty, that is my secret hiding place, and don't you dare ever tell anyone where it is!"

"Scott, I swear it. Your secret cache is safe with me." He knew it would be, because Betty was trust worthy.

In another year, their younger brother, Billy, had grown old enough to join them on Saturday hikes. None of them could explain why the strenuous hikes were so much fun that they would do them again week-after-week. But they knew that each week it was a new adventure and the next time they might discover something new. Maybe Scott would even find a secret artifact time capsule left by an Indian kid many decades ago.

Why did Scott, his sister, and brother like to climb mountains? Their Dad said he knew why: they climbed mountains so they "could see the other side."

15

"SCOTT, JOIN MEADOWLARK IN HER ROW"

It was confusion over dates of school closures for Christmas vacation that caused Scott to attend school for two days at the Cuny Table School on the Pine Ridge Indian Reservation. His friend, Swallow No-Water, had invited him to his home to spend a few days of riding horses together, but the dates became muddled because Scott's school was already closed for Christmas while Swallow's still had two more days to go. When Scott's dad drove him to the reservation and dropped him off at the No-Water home, they did not know that Swallow still had two more days in the classroom.

Scott's dad welcomed the opportunity to go to Cuny Table and visit with Swallow's father, George No-Water, since they had business dealings together. Swallow's father needed a bank loan to purchase some cattle, and Frank McCormick was happy to oblige with a new chunk of potential business. While the men talked alongside the car parked in front, Swallow helped Scott carry a bag with his change of clothes.

"Follow me, Scott. The dog won't bite; he's only getting acquainted." With a dog growling at his heels, Scott was uneasy. "Buster, settle down!" Swallow ordered, and then chased the dog around the corner of the house. "Come in, Scott. Our place may not be as fancy as the Sewright ranch house, but it suits us fine and we like it." The house seemed meager to Scott. A porch was framed with 2x4's and only one window in the front, tar paper sidings, and a corrugated tin roof. Entering the front door, Scott found himself in a large room that was separated into smaller spaces by sliding drapes that hung on wires strung from wall to wall. Open spaces between drapes served as doors. Scott was not surprised since he often visited Bruce Elliot's home in the country south of Buffalo Gap where they also had one large room divided into smaller spaces using sliding drapes. Swallow led the way to a back corner.

"This is my room," he announced. "We'll leave your stuff here and go outside to the corrals and check on the horses. I've got a special one for you. She is a mare named *Paint* that you rode before on the Sewright ranch. It is Meadowlark's pony, but I checked with her and she said it's okay for you to ride it." Scott was happy to hear he had Meadowlark's permission as he remembered her hostile reaction when he rode her pony at the Sewright encampment.

"I'm anxious to see her pony again, but are you sure it's okay with her? Remember last summer when I rode it without her permission, she really took me to task. I thought she was going to slug me," and then he laughed.

"It's okay, trust me. If she gives you any grief, we'll talk to my dad. Now let's get out of here and go to the horse corral."

After Frank McCormick and George No-Water finished their business and McCormick left, it was almost time for supper. Suddenly the front door opened and Meadowlark walked in.

"Hello, Meadowlark," Scott murmured in an offhand way to underplay his excitement to see this pretty Indian girl.

"Scott! What are you doing here?" she blurted out in surprise.

"Didn't you know," he replied. "I'm staying with Swallow for a couple days so we can ride horses."

"You are! Ride horses? Didn't Scott tell you we still have two more days of school? Swallow, did you forget to tell him about that?"

"I guess I forgot, but no big deal," responded Swallow in a rather sheepish manner. "Maybe mother will let me skip the two days until vacation starts. They aren't important."

"That's not likely," Meadowlark countered in a firm voice. "Remember mother told us we can never skip school unless we are sick. Riding horses is no excuse. Scott, I guess you'll just have to go to school with Swallow and me." As she said it she smiled and it was evident she was not disappointed. "You can sit in the desk behind me in our 5th grade row. The teacher, Miss

Two-Bulls won't mind -- one extra student will be okay. We have eight classes in the room, but three of them don't have any students, so one more won't be a problem."

Swallow gave Scott his bed and slept on the floor rolled up in a blanket. Next morning was hectic with the boys up at six, throwing down a quick breakfast and out the door headed to the horse corral. Meadowlark was nowhere to be seen and her dad said he'd drive her to school later since Scott would be riding her pony to school.

"So, we ride ponies to school?" Scott asked as they headed to the horse corral.

"Yeah. Meadowlark and I ride them every day to school. I didn't know our horse riding today would begin so early and with a ride to school, but at least we can have some fun before school.

"How far is it to school?"

"About three miles. It's on the other side of Cuny Table. It normally takes us a little over a half an hour at a fast trot. We'd better get some coats from the house before we leave, because it might be snowing by late afternoon when we have to ride back home."

"Do you and Meadowlark ride to school all year, even in January with snow on the ground?"

"Yeah. It can get cold, but we dress for it. Some mornings with the wind blowing and snow drifting, a horse is about the only way we can get to school. The road would be drifted shut. We don't mind. The coldest part is getting out of bed and heading out the door to the horse corrals. After we get on the pony and start to ride, it gets fun."

The two ponies were mixed in with a half dozen other horses in the corral. Swallow had no problem in placing a halter on the two ponies, then the bridles, and led them the gate where Scott stood. "Remember Paint, she's Meadowlark's pony? You rode her on the Sewright ranch."

"Yeah, I remember. She's a good pony."

"Well, we have to ride bareback; we never use saddles on ponies since they are not big enough to support a saddle." Swallow led his pony out the gate with Scott following. Then he jumped up with his belly across the pony's back and kicking his right leg across to the other side, he sat astride the pony. Scott did it the same way. Together they rode down the dirt road headed to school. It was seven o'clock and they should be there before eight when the school bell would ring. They rode to the horse corral alongside the water tank next to the windmill and hay shed and turned their ponies loose.

When the school bell rang, Scott found himself in the Cuny Table school assigned to the 5th grade row of desks sitting behind Meadowlark. The school was a one-room building that stood by itself in a pasture alongside the dirt road, the only passageway across this high isolated mesa. Two out-house toilets were located in the field behind the school and a shed for firewood leaned up against the back. A windmill in the pasture alongside a water tank turned slowly in the light breeze. Cuny Table was flat as a pool table, a plateau that rose four hundred feet above the surrounding badland terrain. It was six miles long and a half mile wide with steep cliffs on all sides of multi-colored sandstone formations that fell down to the badland's bottom. Crude dirt roads on each end were the only passageways up from the badlands onto the plateau.

The patriarch of the family, Charles Cuny, had established a cattle camp up here on the mesa years ago when the surrounding badlands were considered too barren of vegetation to support a cattle herd, and no one ever climbed up the steep sides of the plateau to discover there was a rich grass field on top. The Cuny family and relatives that numbered several dozen lived in crude houses that were scattered across the landscape. They were all mixed-blood Sioux with a Swiss grandfather who gave the mesa its name. Cuny Table was isolated by twenty miles of harsh badlands terrain from the rest of the Reservation Indians who lived further south near the Indian Agency in the town of Pine Ridge.

There were a dozen students in the Cuny Table School with their desks aligned in three lines. The row closest to the wall included desks for three students in the first grade and two in the second. The middle row had the desks for one in the third grade and three in the fourth. The row next to the window had the desks for Meadowlark in the fifth grade, Swallow in the sixth, plus a desk for a student who was absent.

The teacher, Mary Two-Bulls, was a recent graduate of the teachers college in Chadron, Nebraska, who had been educated in the Reservation school in Oglala. She began the morning by asking all students to face the flag and say the Pledge of Allegiance.

"Students, today we have a visitor from Buffalo Gap who is a guest. Swallow, would you please introduce your guest"

Swallow was caught by surprise since the school had never had a guest before and he didn't know what to say. "Well, Scott is from Buffalo

Gap and came out to ride horses with me, but I didn't remember that we still had school today. So, anyway, Mother made us come to school."

"Hello, Scott," Mary Two-Bulls responded. "We are happy to have you with us. Since you are in the fifth grade in Buffalo Gap, we will let you join Meadowlark in the fifth grade for today. Now we will start classes with the first and second grade who are learning to read and I will be busy with them. The students in the third and fourth grade will go to the blackboard in the front of the room where I have written a number of arithmetic problems, and you will work individually at the blackboard to get the answers. Please, no talking between you." She spoke with a pleasant but firm voice that left no room for nonsense. "Swallow, you can sit at your desk and continue to read the geography book on South America you were reading on Friday. Meadowlark, you can take Scott to the chairs at the back of the room, open you science book, and read chapter six on Biology." She said it in a matter-of-fact manner as if it was no big deal; Scott's reaction was panic! He sat stunned. Reading a book together with Meadowlark, and on the subject of biology?

Meadowlark arose from her desk, turned to Scott with a knowing smile and announced: "Come on, Scott, we'll go to the back of the room and you can read with me." She said it as if reading a book together with a boy her own age from Buffalo Gap was a normal thing to do -- and was obviously enjoying it. She wore a bright yellow, tight-fitting blouse that was in contrast with her long black hair that fell to her shoulders and her dark eyes that sparkled with the reflections from the sunshine that streaked through the window. Scott was flustered.

Scott followed her to the back of the room where she had pulled two chairs up against each other. She sat on one and waited for Scott to sit down, which he did tentatively. Then she slid her chair even closer to Scott and opened the book, which she placed on her lap. He looked at the book. The page was open to Chapter Six: Biology. It was not a subject he knew anything about, but it seemed to be an embarrassing subject about sex and things like that. How was he going to survive sitting next to a pretty girl and reading together about biology?

With the book on her lap, she used her finger as a pointer and began to read in a whisper:

"Biology is a science that studies life and living things, including their origin, growth, and evolution. It often begins with a look at the cell, the basis of life..."

Scott could not concentrate on what was being said as her shoulder brushed up against him. She was so close he could smell the aroma of the soap she had washed her face with that morning. He was uneasy. Looking over his shoulder, he saw Swallow at his desk reading his book.

"Come on, Scott," she whispered. "Pay attention. You and I are supposed to be reading the chapter about biology."

"Meadowlark, I don't know anything about biology," he whispered. "I've never heard anything about it before. Anyway, I'm nervous reading about biology with a girl."

"Don't be silly," she whispered back in an exasperated voice. "I'm just a girl. Pretend that I'm a boy like Swallow and he's reading it with you."

"But you don't sound like Swallow and you are not a boy. You are a pretty girl and I am nervous."

"Do you really think I am pretty?"

"Wow!

"Do you really?"

"Yes."

"How pretty?" She asked it in a teasing manner. " Am I as pretty as Shirley Temple?"

"Yeah, I guess. I don't know much about Shirley Temple, but I guess she must be pretty too."

"Scott, whisper. We've got to keep reading or Miss Two-Bulls will get upset. Now settle down and follow my finger."

By the third page, Miss Two-Bulls had finished with the first and second grades and was at the black board with the third and fourth grades and going over their arithmetic exercises. Then it was time for the morning recess.

"Come on, Scott," announced Meadowlark, closing the biology book, and taking his hand to lead him back to his desk. She was holding his hand? -- He dropped into the desk, shaken with the sudden hand holding. "You and I and Swallow can go outside. Put on your coat. It's not too cold to ride on the swings." She seemed to be ordering him around as if she owned him, and he didn't mind at all. Swallow closed his book and the three of them headed out the door for recess.

At noon, they ate sandwiches Meadowlark had brought from home sitting on chairs at the back of the room while Miss Two-Bulls sat at her desk eating her lunch in the front corner of the room.

Then it began to snow. Looking out the window, they could see the flakes starting to come down.

Swallow raised his voice so the teacher could hear. "Miss Two-Bulls, could Meadowlark, Scott and I be excused to leave for the day? We have to ride horses home, and would like to get started before the snow gets too heavy."

There was an immediate response from the teacher. "Yes, Swallow, you can leave to go home. But you said Meadowlark is leaving with you. You only have two ponies?"

"That's okay. Two of us can ride double – we've done it before and the ponies are used to it."

Swallow, Meadowlark, and Scott put on their coats and hats and headed out the door and walked to the horse corral. Swallow placed the bridles on the ponies. It was snowing and the wind was beginning to howl.

"Scott, you'll have to ride double with Meadowlark in front so she can hold the reins, with you sitting in back. The pony is used to her handling the reins so she should do it." He jumped on his pony and led the way out the gate.

"Okay, Scott," said Meadowlark. "I'll get on first, then you jump on behind and hang on to me. That's how we ride double."

With that brief instruction, she jumped onto the back of the pony and sat waiting for Scott to get on. He was in shock! Riding double with a girl?

"Meadowlark, I've never rode double before. You'll have to help me and tell me how."

"Climb up on the fence rail, reach your leg behind me over the back of Paint, and just sit down behind me; it's easy."

Scott did as he was told, and found himself sitting on the pony crushed up against the back of Meadowlark. "Now put your arms around me and hang on," she instructed in a matter-of-fact manner. "Hang on tight, because I'm going to start to gallop to catch up with Swallow."

He almost fell off as the pony started to run, so he grabbed ahold and tightened his arms around Meadowlark. Her hair was in his face. It smelled nice. As the horse galloped, they bounced up and down together and he could feel his body rubbing against her hind end. The snow was coming down more heavily now, causing him to close his eyes and hang on. He hoped Meadowlark and the horse could see the road ahead.

99

"How are you doing, Scott?" she asked as she turned her head to look at him, and her face touched his. She left it there against him for a minute and smiled. He felt her cheek against him – it felt nice; but it was cold from the driving snow.

"I'm doing okay, I guess. How are you doing?"

"Great. Isn't this great? I love riding in the snow. This is the first time I've ever rode double in a snowstorm. Isn't it fun?"

"I guess so, Meadowlark. I know it must be hard seeing ahead with the snow and wind in your face, but I hope you can see okay."

"I don't need to see much. Paint knows the way. Hang on tight and we'll be home before long; only another mile to go."

Scott felt reassured. Meadowlark had so much spunk and poise, she gave him confidence. He began to enjoy the pony ride with this beautiful Indian girl riding in front, so he placed his arms around her more tightly to hang on. She didn't seem to mind.

When they arrived at the No-Water home, Scott's father's car was parked in front. He was inside waiting for their return from school. When it started to snow in Buffalo Gap, he asked his wife to manage the bank and headed to Cuny Table, knowing that the road up onto the mesa would be closed shortly – possibly for days.

Swallow and Meadowlark were standing at the door waving as Scott drove away. Swallow and he would have a lot to talk about next summer at the tipi encampment on Beaver Creek. He hoped Meadowlark would be there.

CURSE OF BEAR BUTTE

The camping trip began at daybreak. The three boys followed Joe Norman to the barn where hired-hand Mike had already loaded the tent, camping gear, and provisions on the two mules named *Hardware* and *Turntable*. They saddled their horses and headed out with Rex in front followed by Swallow and Scott leading the two mules.

The camping trip was in the planning phase for weeks. The original idea was hatched by the boys but tirelessly pursued by the fathers, who became enthusiastically involved. It became a rite-of-passage for the sons as a crusade to rediscover their family roots: starting with the Norman ranch, settled by Joe's ancestors before the turn of the century; a *pah-Ha SAH-pah* homecoming for No-Water in the heritages of his Sioux nation; and a sentimental visit to the Cuyhoga Gold Mine where Frank McCormick was raised. Each father had a vicarious rendezvous with nostalgia.

With the help of their fathers, every detail of the ten day trip had been planned: the route, camping sites, and menus. It was a risk for three teenage boys to head out by themselves unsupervised, but the fathers had all faced greater challenges during their own youth. For additional safety, Frank McCormick had contacted the head of Custer State Park, a childhood friend of his, to keep an eye on the boys as they proceeded through the heart of the Black Hills.

The first day's route was easy, mostly alongside established dirt roads:

up Lame Johnny creek, through the town of Buffalo Gap, beyond the narrow buffalo gap to the Streeter ranch, and to a pasture on the Sanson's ranch where Frank McCormick had made arrangements with Carl Sanson for the boys to camp for a night.

Setting up camp the first evening was easy because everything was well organized in the packs on the mule's back. Rex took the lead in pitching the tent; it was an ancient relic of his father's. Shafts on the ends held up a center pole; canvas was stretched across the top and pulled out on the sides with guy ropes tied to stakes; and flaps hung in front and back. Scott cooked the evening meal over a camp fire enclosed with rocks, demonstrating his cooking skill from the Boy Scouts. The menu called for steak and potatoes. Swallow removed the packs from the mules, watered the horses, and picketed them in a grassy meadow nearby. It was a beautiful clear night with coyotes on a nearby mountain top howling at a full moon. The boys rolled up in their blankets early, tired from the hard day's twenty-five mile ride, and were fast asleep.

The second day carried them into the heart of the Black Hills. Climbing up the mile-long McCurran grade to the grassland meadows, they encountered their first buffalo herd. It contained a hundred bulls and cows that grazed slowly along and ignored the three riders and two mules that passed along its edge. Buffalo had replaced the cattle that grazed here in previous years. Orrin McCurran was a customer of his dad's at the bank until his cattle ranch had been purchased by Custer State Park, forcing McCurran to move elsewhere. Now the ranch buildings and fences had been removed and the land returned to nature and bison herds.

By late afternoon they had reached Flynn Creek and followed along it for several miles to the beaver dams. Scott had fished there with his father, and a nearby meadow was often the locale of a McCormick family Sunday picnic. Before establishing camp, the boys decided to fish in the beaver dams because they saw trout jumping. Tying their horses to a tree and staking-out the mules, they became engrossed as they fished the beaver dams in the pursuit of trout for an evening meal.

Suddenly, Crash! Boom! The roar of thunder! A blinding flash of lightning simultaneously hit a nearby tree. The sky had turned a deep purple – a violent storm unexpectedly hit. Even before they could crawl off the beaver dams, they were hit with sheets of water driven by a furious storm front. They rushed to a nearby tree to huddle in its shelter. The rain came down in torrents, drenching them. Blinding lightning flashes and thunder sonic booms radiated through the forest.

"My God!" yelled Scott. "We've got to move out from under this tree or we may get hit by lightning!"

"Move where?" shouted Rex. "There's no place else to go."

"We can't stay here under a tree with lightning everywhere."

Suddenly they were standing knee-deep in water.

"We might get hit by a flash flood if the beaver dams break," hollered Swallow. "Where can we go?"

They continued to huddle together behind a tree as the storm increased in fury. They were soaked to the skin and cold.

"Quick, we've got to help the horses," shouted Rex. "They're terrified of lightning and will pull up their stakes and stampede. We've got to lead them to safety and tie them up." He ran through the bombarding rain to where the frightened horses were tugging at their picket ropes. The mules had already pulled free and run into the woods.

Swallow and Scott followed Rex on a dead run and grabbed the halter ropes of their horses. The terrified horses were riotous. Rex got his horse under a tree and tied it up. He chased after a run-away mule, caught his halter rope, and tied him to a tree. The other mule was nowhere to be seen in the pelting rain and darkness. He helped Scott and Swallow with their horses; they huddled together under a tree talking about what to do. They were drenched and getting colder, and the storm gave no indication of letting-up.

"My God! This is a cyclone," screamed Rex. "I hear trees getting blown down. If we stay here, we may be killed. We've got to get out of here."

"Hey, I remember an abandon hay barn out in the middle of the meadow," Scott roared. "It may have a roof and give us some protection. It's a half mile. We've got to run for it."

"Good idea, Scott," declared Rex. "You know where it is; lead the way."

"Follow me," shouted Scott. He sprang to his feet and raced in the descending darkness down the Flynn Creek draw followed by the other two boys. Rivulets of rising water over their knees were everywhere. They sprinted at top speed, not knowing which torrent may be bottomless. The ground was covered with a blanket of hail, and water was everywhere. Each inlet had become a dangerous swirl of a rushing river. The boys splashed through them at full speed following Scott, who hoped he could remember where the barn was located. Flashes of lightning were the only light. Suddenly Scott saw the outlines of the barn in the distance. They raced to it. The barn had been abandoned and the doors were wide open. The boys dashed inside and into total darkness.

Suddenly, with the protection of the old structure, they were out of the rain. Except for the lightning they were in total darkness, but could feel loose hay under their feet. Moving to the lee side with fewest roof leaks, they sat down in the soft hay. They were out of the rain, and even though they were drenched, they felt secure in a dry place. It would be a long, endless night, but they could survive.

In the morning, Scott was the first to stir. He had dozed off-and-on for several hours. When he saw the first rays of sunlight shining through the cracks in the barn sides, he rose to his feet and tentatively explored the barn interior. There was little to discover: four walls, a partial roof, and a layer of hay on the dirt floor. He walked to the open door and looked out. He was shocked at what he saw – the barn was enclosed by an enormous herd of bison on all sides. They were surrounded.

"Rex, Swallow, wake up!" he yelled. "My God! We are surrounded by bison. They're on all sides of us, a hundreds of them. Come take a look. What are we going to do?"

Rex got to his feet and came to his side and looked out the door. "My God! Scott, I see what you mean. Swallow, come and look at this."

"My God!" exclaimed Swallow. "I've never seen so many bison before; I didn't know there were so many. What are we going to do? I don't know if it's safe to walk through a herd of bison. Guys, what do you think?"

"I don't know either," said Scott, "but I think we'll have to find out. They are between us and our horses. Maybe if we are quiet and just start walking slowly toward the meadow, they will ignore us just like that herd did yesterday on McCurran Hill."

"Yeah," responded Rex, "I think that's what we'll have to do, and probably the sooner the better before the herd starts to stir. Some of the bulls are still lying down, so if we're lucky and quiet, they may pay us no attention."

"Okay, Rex, you lead the way and Scott and I will follow. Walk slowly, but I'm going to keep my eyes on the nearest tree and be prepared to do some fast climbing if I see a bull getting excited and coming after me."

"Okay, follow me," said Rex as he stepped out the barn door. Together the three boys walked slowly through the herd. As they had hoped, the bison paid them no heed.

They reached the horses and a mule, but the other mule was nowhere to be seen.

"*Hardware* is still here, but only God knows where *Turntable* may have run off to during the lightning storm," Rex said. "And *Turntable* is the mule with all our food. Damn, we could do without *Hardware* and the tents she carries, but we can't survive long without the food in *Turntable's* pack."

"Rex, what are we going to do?" asked Swallow.

"I guess we'll have to go hunting for *Turntable*."

"Yeah! We don't have too many options," responded Scott. "Someone should stay here at a camp while the other two ride horses in opposite directions and see if anyone can pick up a trail or be lucky and find the mule when it stopped running. I've got a couple candy bars in my saddle bag that we can share for breakfast. If you guys want to ride, I'll stay here, set up camp and see if I can catch some fish for us to eat. Every time I've fished here with my dad we always caught fish."

"Good program, Scott," said Rex. "Swallow, you head south toward the McCurran ranch along the way we came yesterday. I will go north in the direction of Mount Coolidge." If we don't find anything by noon when the sun is directly overhead, then we should both head back to our camp and get here before dark. Scott, I hope you catch some fish, because I sure will be hungry by suppertime."

With the outline of that plan, Rex and Swallow mounted their horses and headed out. Scott lifted the tent out of *Hardware's* pack and began to set it up. Then, grabbing his fish pole, he went to the beaver dams to fish. Underneath stones he found worms and grubs that he used for bate. It was the most intense fishing he had ever done because the trout he caught would be their only source of food. He saw large frogs lying on the banks of the beaver dam and managed to catch several of them to grill with the fish.

Then he remembered things from the Wilderness Survival Merit Badge he had studied in Boy Scouts. Water cress was growing in the beaver dams and he remembered his dad telling him they ate it when he was a little boy as a salad; so, he picked a batch to go with the fish and frog legs. While picking the water cress, he also saw wild onions growing along the sides of Flynn Creek and knew from the Merit Badge that it was good to eat, so he picked some. He would chop-up the onions and add it to the water cress. Since he had no cooking utensils – they were in the missing pack – he would have to improvise. Cutting willows, he made a grill with the fish and frog legs contained between two sides tied together. He would mount it over the camp fire. When the other guys returned, they could have an evening meal of salad and grilled trout with frog legs.

In the late afternoon Rex and Swallow returned, having ridden many miles with no success in finding the lost mule. Famished, they ate the meal Scott had prepared. As darkness fell, they crawled under their blankets in the tent. Their stomachs were full from a hearty meal, and they were dry; but they were tired and quickly fell asleep.

Early the next morning they took down the tent, climbed on their horses and headed north in the direction of Mount Coolidge, which they could see several miles in the distance. Rex and Scott rode ahead and Swallow led the mule. They had traveled a couple miles when in the distance they saw a man in a ranger uniform on a horse headed their way and leading a mule, their *Turntable*.

"Howdy, boys," he declared as he pulled to a stop and faced the three young men. "I'll bet one of you is named Scott McCormick."

"Yes sir," responded Scott. "I'm Scott McCormick. How did you know?"

"Well, boys, I am Jim Thorpe, the head of Custer State Park, and I've been looking for you. Scott, your father and I have known each other since we were in school together in Custer. He told me you were headed this way and I've been expecting you. After the cyclone on Flynn Creek, we've been worried and were out looking for you. Found your mule half way up Mount Coolidge."

"Hooray!" replied Scott. "That mule ran away during the storm frightened from the lightning and it had all our food in his pack. He left us with nothing to eat. Thank God you found him."

"Are you guys okay? That cyclone cut through the park from McCurran Hill to Flynn Creek. It was a mean one and you were at its center. There was flash flooding in all the draws and dozens of trees blown over. I had the itinerary your dad sent me that indicated you were in the vicinity of the storm. So I came looking for you. On the way I found your mule with his pack still on. I was worried about you. Glad to find you here and in good shape. I've got some extra food with me, so let me give it to you. It may not be a great breakfast, but it will fill your bellies." He handed each a packet of biscuits.

"Thank you, Mister Thorpe. My dad always talks about you. I'm sure glad you came looking for us and that you found our mule. Yes, it was a bad storm; the worse we've ever seen. We managed to make it to that old abandoned barn in the middle of the Flynn Creek meadow and spend the night there. The only problem was we found ourselves barricaded inside by a herd of Bison. We had to walk through them next morning to get to our horses."

"You guys sure are lucky. You survived a cyclone, the worse storm we've seen in the park in years, and then you were surrounded and walked through a herd of bison." Then he smiled. "I guess you all must be carrying a rabbit's foot. Anyway, boys, glad to see you are all unhurt and safe. Now, let's turn around and travel together to Blue Bell Lodge where I've parked my pickup and horse trailer. From the lodge we can call your dad, Scott, because he is worried about you."

After arriving at the lodge with Thorpe, the boys continued on their journey. Two days later, their caravan arrived at the Cuyhoga Gold Mine where Scott's dad had spent his youth. The only remaining evidence at the mine shaft was an opening into the mountain that was barricaded by the Forest Service for safety to keep everyone out. Nearby in a meadow alongside Iron Mountain Creek stood a tumbledown log cabin with the roof caved-in and the doors and windows all missing. This was the home where Frank McCormick had spent his youth. Further up the hillside were ruins of several other mine buildings and a small shack, the former assay office. Scott had visited Cuyhoga when hiking in with his father, and he knew the history well. They pitched their tent in the meadow and set up camp. It was still early afternoon, so they decided to ride a mile north to the top of Iron Mountain where they could see the mountain carving called Mount Rushmore. Riding over the crest of the hill, they saw it in the distance and were in awe. Dismounting, they tied their horses to a tree and sat on a granite ledge to admire the scene. It was breathtaking. The profile of President Washington was closest to them with President Lincoln on the far side. Between the two were two other faces only partially completed; Scott knew they would become Jefferson and Teddy Roosevelt.

Scott commented, "Wow! Isn't that view great. Think about it, our presidents carved in granite as big and high as a mountain and there for everyone to see for hundreds of years."

"Yes," replied Rex. "It sure is impressive."

Swallow sat in silence. Then Scott remembered that Sioux Indians may not share the same reverence for United States Presidents as he and Rex. "Swallow, I hear that someday they are going to carve a mountain down near Custer in the image of Chief Crazy Horse. So someday your people will also have something to celebrate."

"Yeah," responded swallow without much enthusiasm. "That will be nice, if it ever happens."

The boys mounted their horses and rode down Iron Mountain back to their camp alongside Iron Creek at the Cuyhoga mine.

Next morning they broke camp to head to their final destination, which was a special request of Swallow's grandfather, No-Water. It was to climb Bear Butte, *mah-TOH pah-HA*, where the old warrior had seen visions of the White Buffalo in better times. It would be a hard two-day ride to get there traveling north in the direction of Deadwood then veering off to the right down through Elm Canyon and onto the plains south of Sturgis. They skirted the town of Sturgis and passed through Fort Meade, then established their camp on the eastern side of the Bear Butte.

Bear Butte stands by itself alone as a symbolic sentinel to all Indians on the prairie protecting the eastern edge of the Black Hills and separated from it by a couple miles. It is a steep pyramid on all sides except for a ridge on the east; rising twelve hundred feet above the surrounding prairie. From earliest times, it has been a sacred mountain to Indian tribes, first the Cheyenne who originally occupied the Dakota plains and later the Sioux who became dominate. To the Indians it was the place where *Ma'her'o* (God) imparted a prophet from which they derived their religious customs. It is a sacred mountain to Indians of many tribes who make pilgrimages to place prayer cloths and relics tied to the branches of trees along the mountain's flanks. For the few who can reach the top, religious ceremonies are performed there.

Swallow had been sent as an emissary from his grandfather to climb to the top and pay homage to his vision of the White Buffalo, which No-Water had experienced many decades before when he was a member of Sitting Bull's nomad tribe. While Swallow did not share the same sacred feeling of his grandfather about Bear Butte, he wanted to show respect and to honor No-Water's Indian roots.

"Guy's I've got to climb to the top of Bear Butte," he announced. "You guys don't have to do it, so I can make the climb alone; it is a promise I made to my grandfather. I have to leave a prayer cloth and other relics he gave me tied to a tree on the summit. The mountain is sacred to Indians, it is a religious shrine."

"Heck, Swallow, do you think we'd let you go alone?" countered Scott. "Rex and I are going to climb it with you. Your grandfather, No-Water, is a friend of mine from his time in the tipi encampment on the Sewright ranch. Did he give you any indication of what route to follow to get to the top? It looks nearly impossible and I don't see an easy way up. There probably isn't any trail. I don't think anyone could climb it from the West side. Maybe we can get up the eastern side that is more gradual near the bottom, but even that gets mighty steep higher up."

The boys were up early and after a quick breakfast they rode their horses partway up the eastern slope to a saddle in a ridge where huge rock cliffs dominated the landscape. They tied their horses to a tree and set-out on foot. The first part of the climb was a deer trail through the trees. During this part of the climb, they encountered two rattlesnakes lying in the trail and sidestepped both without danger. After another two hours of strenuous climbing, they reached the four thousand foot level and could see the summit four hundred feet above them.

The going became even more difficult. Above them was the erosion of sedimentary strata and igneous rock that lay loosely scattered on the steep hillside. Each rock when dislodged flew down like a projective, a danger to anyone below. Every two steps climbed resulted in a rock slide backward losing a step, so progress was slow. There was no trail or outcropping to give footing. Shortly before noon they reached the summit, took water from their canteens and ate a candy bar.

The summit had a flat area a half- acre in size and it was covered with shrub pine trees. Brightly colored prayer clothes were tied to many of the branches. While Scott and Rex rested in the shade of a tree, Swallow disappeared, and they figured he was engaged in his grandfather's ritual with the prayer clothes and relics. As they sat resting, Scott noticed that his hair was beginning to rise on end, and he felt a tingling around his head. My God! He wondered if this was static electrical charge encountered on hot mountain tops and the danger they had been warned about. He looked to the south and saw the telltale signs of dark purple clouds. He knew the signs of impending peril from their experience at Flynn Creek.

"You guys!" he yelled. "We've got to get off the mountain and out of here. Now! A lightning storm is about to hit."

Even before they could react, a bolt of lightning hit a tree on the summit accompanied by the crash of thunder. The storm had arrived. Suddenly sheets of rain blasted them. Swallow came running and together they plunged over the edge of the summit and down the northern slope, slipping on the loose rocks that cascaded below them in rock slides. Bolts of lightning flashed as trees on the summit were hit, accompanied with the crash of thunder. They became drenched in the driving rain and wind gushes pushed them down the steep slope. With no footholds, their feet slid out-of-control downward in the loose gravel. In a matter of minutes they were near the end of the steepest part.

Suddenly Scott heard a yell from Swallow. Looking back, he saw him rolling head-over-heels down the slope then sliding to a stop on his stomach. Swallow managed to roll over to his butt and sit up.

"Are you okay," yelled Scott.

"Yeah, but my ankle is hurt. I think I sprained it or maybe it's broken."

"Don't move. I'll be back up there to help you." Scott found difficulty in the driving rain regaining the slope back to where Swallow sat. Gusts of wind blew him backward. "Swallow, take off your boot and let me see that ankle."

Swallow winched as he slowly removed the boot.

"It doesn't seem too bad," announced Scott after an examination. "I don't think anything is broken. Maybe it's just a sprain. We'll put your boot back on and use my shirt as a support bandage. I'll wrap it around your ankle and boot like a splint so your foot can't move."

Rex had climbed back up to join them.

"Rex, get under his left arm and I'll take the other. We'll get him to his feet and go down together. It can't be too far to the horses. Swallow, keep your bad foot raised and let Rex and I support you."

It was slow going as the three slid together virtually arm-in-arm down the mountain slope in the treacherous footing, pushed by the driving rain and gusting wind. In another half hour they reached the horses. Back at the camp, the ground was nearly dry. The storm was confined to only the summit and slopes of Bear Butte.

"Don't you guys laugh," said Swallow. "But I think we just witnessed the bewitched curse of Bear Butte. Sixty years ago my Grandfather was nearly done-in on that mountain, and today it almost happened to me."

"Yeah, Swallow," responded Scott. "The same thing happened to both you and your grandfather. I think that mountain has it in for you Indians – at least the No-Water tribe. Rex and I both got off it without any harm, just wet as hell. Anyway, Swallow, we made it down and I don't care about ever climbing it again. Once is enough. But if I ever do go up there again, I won't go with any No-Water."

The next morning they broke camp, placed everything in the packs on the mules, and headed to Fort Meade where they were scheduled to meet their fathers. It was Sunday morning and they had been on the trail for ten days. Rex's father arrived pulling a horse trailer and Swallow's dad would ride home in the car with Frank McCormick.

The boys were tired and ready to sit quietly and ride in a comfortable automobile on the homeward trail. As he climbed in the car, George No-Water asked Scott what he thought about the climb of Bear Butte.

"Well, sir, it was awesome. But I will never climb it again. I don't want any of that No-Water curse to wash off on me. Once is enough."

RELIGION WASN'T AN ISSUE
IN BUFFALO GAP

When someone would ask Scott what religion he was, he'd say Catholic, even though he spent more time in the Methodist than the Catholic Church – and he did not particularly like spending time on Sunday in any church.

Scott inherited his religion. His dad was raised Catholic, or was a Catholic in name, and inherited his religion from his father, Scott's grandfather. They lived in the wilds of the Black Hills far from any church and seldom attended Mass. Scott's mother was raised a Methodist by her family, but resented the restrictions placed on her by a religion that permitted no card-playing or dancing; so at the time of her marriage she was agreeable to have any children raised as Catholic. Their religious differences were easy to accommodate in Camp Crook where they made their first home, because the town had neither a Catholic nor Methodist church.

When the family moved to Buffalo Gap, they found the Catholic Church was served by a missionary priest who travelled to town only every third week. The priest kept the children in the pews after Mass to be drilled in the Baltimore Catechism, the official doctrine of the church. The other two Sundays, the children attended the Methodist Church where they learned the Protestant Saint James Bible from a Sunday School Teacher.

Religion was not a factor in the Buffalo Gap public schools that Scott attended, nor much of an issue anyplace else in town. During the difficult years of the 1930's Great Depression, people had enough to worry about from day-to-day to spend much time worrying about a destination in the after-life.

When the Methodist's hosted an Oyster Supper at their church, everyone in town attended, including all the Episcopalians and Catholics – of which there were only Scott's family and a dozen others. When the Catholics held their annual Saint Patrick's dance in the auditorium, everyone in town – plus all the ranchers and cowboys from miles around – attended and danced until 2 am, when the missionary priest decided it was time for him to head back to the rectory in Hermosa. Buffalo Gap was an equal opportunity religious community before that became fashionable nationwide during World War Two. People tried to do what was right and live as a good neighbor, treating others the way they would also like to be treated. Of course, that did not apply to everyone; some had never heard of the 'Golden Rule' and tended to ignore what it stood for.

All of this was beyond the grasp of Scott. He did what his father and mother told him to do – at least most of the time. He also believed what they told him to believe; no point in having to figure things out by one's self. There were plenty of other things to contemplate, and he could save some things for when he got older; at least, that's the way it seemed to him.

18

"A DATE WHICH WILL LIVE IN INFAMY!"

Scott did not know on Sunday morning that the day would become historic and different from all the rest that were to follow; it was the beginning of World War Two.

Rex had come with his parents from the ranch to spend Sunday in Buffalo Gap with his aunt and uncle. Scott and Rex spent the morning exploring things in the barns and corrals and looking at the horses. In mid-afternoon they walked into the Sewright living room to find the adults huddled around the radio listening to a news broadcast.

"Unknown planes are dropping bombs on Pearl Harbor," the radio blared. "They carry the marking of Japanese planes, and they are strafing people on the ground and Hickam airfield. Many people have been killed. Torpedo planes and dive bombers are dropping missiles on American battleships. Some of our ships are on fire; flames and smoke fill the sky."

This sounded serious. Scott and Rex stopped to listen. What was going on? The adults were glued to the radio and could not answer the boy's questions, because no one knew what was happening. As he listened, Scott slowly pieced the news story together. Japanese airplanes were bombing our American ships in Pearl Harbor, Hawaii. That means the Japanese have started a war against America. Even though he had heard news reports for the previous year about the fighting going on in Europe against Germany and Italy, he never paid any attention because it did not affect America. But now we were in a war against the Japanese! Who were the Japanese?

"Goddamn Japs!" shouted Joe Norman. "A sneak attack against America! We'll show those goddamn slimy, slant-eyed bastards a thing or two! Who do they think they are that they can take us on?"

"Yeah! We'll show them!" added Pop Bill Sewright. "They've bit off more than they can chew."

"Does that mean that now we'll have to fight both the Japanese and the German's?" asked Florence Sewright. "So far we've managed to stay out of the war in Europe. Now, will we have to fight against all of them – the Japanese, the German's, and the Italians? Dear Lord, I hope it doesn't mean that. I hope not. I lost my brother, Johnny, fighting against the Germans in the last war."

"Goddamn Japs!" shouted Joe Norman again. "Slimy bastards, we'll show them a thing or two. Yeah, we'll take them all on – the Germans, Italians, and the damn Japs. We might as well get three for the price of one."

Scott and Rex listened for a while, and then returned to the barn. But Scott was worried. "What if the Japanese came in over the hills out of Calico Canyon from west of town and attacked Buffalo Gap shooting people? Rex, we'd better be ready. I'd get my Dad's shotgun and dig a fox hole on top of Reservoir Hill. You could get your Dad's thirty-thirty rifle and join me. Together we might be able to hold them off from getting into town."

"Yeah! But Scott, we'd probably be terribly out-numbered."

"If we had to, we could fall back and establish a skirmish line along the highway a block west of my home. There is a deep irrigation ditch there we could fight from. Some of the men from town could join us. I wonder what kind of fighters they are – those Japs? I'll bet they probably aren't very good. Maybe we could get some air support with air planes from Rapid City and drop bombs on them"

Scott and Rex were deadly serious in preparing to fight a war. They had become frightened as they listened to the news broadcasts that extended late into Sunday night. Everyone was sitting next to a radio and listening for the latest news. Japanese airplanes were dropping bombs on American battleships and killing Americans. Where was Hawaii? Scott had never heard of it and didn't know where it was. If it could happen in

Hawaii, it could happen anywhere – even in Buffalo Gap. The Japanese had suddenly become their enemy and a focus of Scott's life.

The next morning, Scott listened to President Roosevelt on the radio as he addressed the United States Congress.

"Yesterday, December 7th, 1941 – a date which will live in infamy— the United States of America was suddenly and deliberately attacked by naval and air forces of the Empire of Japan. ... The attack was deliberately planned many days or even weeks ago. During the intervening time the Japanese Government had deliberately sought to deceive the United States by false statements and expressions of hope for continued peace. ... The attack yesterday on the Hawaiian Islands has caused severe damage to American naval and military forces. Very many American lives have been lost. .. Yesterday the Japanese Government also launched an attack against Malaya. ... Last night they attacked Hong Kong. ... Guam, Philippine Islands, Wake Island, Midway Island, a surprise offensive extending throughout the Pacific area. ... As commander-in-chief of the Army and Navy, I have directed that all measures be taken for our defense."

Then President Roosevelt concluded his address to the Congress: "With confidence in our armed forces – with the unbounding determination or our people – we will gain the inevitable triumph – so help us God!"

Immediately after his address, the Congress of the United States declared war against Japan, Germany and Italy. Scott's country was now at war!

Nothing in the future would ever be the same. Scott's world was suddenly turned upside down. Soon there was gas rationing, which meant little travel anywhere such as no Sunday picnics in the Black Hills; food was rationed; virtually everyone moved away from Buffalo Gap to work elsewhere in defense industries; and all the young men were drafted into the army. Buffalo Gap became a ghost town.

Scott lost his saddle pals. Rex moved to Rapid City. Swallow and his family left the reservation to live somewhere else. Scott was not to see Meadowlark again until after the war.

His family moved away too. Scott's high school years were spent elsewhere during the uneasy era of World War Two.

Before the moving van pulled away, he crossed the dirt road to the Sewright corral where Buck stood with his head reaching over the fence.

Scott patted his forehead and with tears in his eyes said, "Thanks old friend, you helped me become a real cowboy."

At least he had those wonderful times of his boyhood years. They may all be in the past, but he has the memories of when he became a cowboy – a real man. Maybe someday in the future he would see his saddle pals again: that would be awesome!

ABOUT THE AUTHOR

This is Bernie Keating's ninth book. His eclectic writing pursuits include books on frontier history, religion, music, economics, science, and two novels.

He was raised in Buffalo Gap, South Dakota, the setting for this novel. In his youth he had the aspiration to become a cowboy and ride the open range; however, as an adult he became an executive with a major multinational company and rode airplanes around the world.

In a throwback to his youth, he and his wife now live on a ranch in the Sierra Mountains near Sonora, California, where they raise maverick deer and stray cats.